This Is Where We Live

This Is Where We Live

Kate Hardie

4th ESTATE • London

4th Estate
An imprint of HarperCollins*Publishers*
1 London Bridge Street
London SE1 9GF

www.4thestate.co.uk

HarperCollins*Publishers*
Macken House, 39/40 Mayor Street Upper,
Dublin 1, D01 C9W8, Ireland

First published in Great Britain in 2023 by 4th Estate

1

Typeset in Walbaum MT Std by
Palimpsest Book Production Ltd, Falkirk, Stirlingshire

Printed and Bound in the UK using 100% Renewable Electricity
at CPI Group (UK) Ltd

This book is produced from independently certified FSC™ paper
to ensure responsible forest management.

For more information visit: www.harpercollins.co.uk/green

For my mum and my child,
thank you for the love and courage.

Note: In this book there is talk of self-harm and harm to others. Unsafe parenting and scared children. Suicide, transphobia, misgendering, birth trauma and post-natal depression. Broken families and absent fathers.

I hope that is not all there is in this book or that this is all you will be left with if you choose to carry on reading. But I don't want your hurt and personal history ambushed or triggered without warning and I wish you strength and support with all you carry.

1

WHEN THEY WERE BORN THEY SLEPT ON MY CHEST. THEIR tiny heart beating against mine. Their skin smelling of milk, sour poo and warm. Their chipolata arms spread over me like open wings. Their face pressed sideways, their cheek on my breast. While they puffed out sleep and I lay awake, nervous. My sweet sleeping child.

And I listened to their breathing. And I wanted to protect them. From cold and heat and hunger. From zombies and heartbreak. From floods and no more bees. From burns and boredom. From missing their stop. From losing their marbles, murder and sickness. From rain and wind, dirt in their wounds and sand in their eyes.

From thoughtless teachers and cruel friends. From cuts and sores and scratches and poisons. From fools and flirts and all the other chancers. From hopelessness and the days when the dark won't lift.

I wanted to hold them on my chest forever and keep everything bad away, but most of all I wanted to protect them from me.

2

M Y MOUTH TASTES OF BLOOD AND BONE. THERE'S RAW ripped flesh between my teeth. My back aches. There's torn skin and drying blood under my fingernails.

I'm naked. Curled up in the corner of my bedroom. I've slept on the floor. The soles of my feet have dirt and grazes all over them. My head is thumping, like a spoon is smashing down on me, like I'm a big boiled egg.

I know I have done terrible things. I know I am hateful and hated.

My child calls out from their room: 'Mum, are you awake? Are you OK?'

I call back, 'I'm OK, my love.'

They're thirteen now, daily disappearing away from me in a snarl of disapproval.

'I need to go to school.'

I push myself up from the floor, my hand slipping in a puddle of my own wee. I grab a nightie out of the laundry bin and use it as a mop, chucking it dripping back on the bin edge, little puddles of pee pooling on the floor below. I'll deal with it later.

I flop down onto my bed and pretend that I slept there. 'I know, love. Do you have everything you need? There's jam in the fridge.'

'I don't like jam any more, I told you!'

'OK, sorry, love.' My spine aches like it's crumbling.

There's a rope tying us together, invisible but strong, frayed but it stays knotted.

They haven't gone. I can hear their breath, smell their musty hair and three-day-worn socks. I can't tell them how to dress anymore. They're asserting their right to choose. Their right to wear stinky socks if that's what they want. They're gearing up to making bigger choices. Ones I will also have no say in.

They push the door open. I pull up the duvet. It's cold when it should be warm. Nobody slept in here last night. They stand there, leaning their head against the door frame, staring at me. They want to say something but I'm not sure they know what it is and I don't ask.

I glance at my hands. Bloodstains on my palms. I pull them under the cover.

'You OK, Mum?'

Yes, for now, yes, for you, no, not really. You know I'm not.

'Yes. Do you want me to walk you to school?'

'Yeah, maybe, if that's OK.'

'Give me a minute to get dressed. Go and make me some toast.'

They grunt a response and go.

A bruise like an aubergine blossoming on my thigh, dark and mean. I push my finger into it to feel the ache. I go to the sink, spit dried blood and a bit of skin. Turn on the tap, watch it spin a red ribbon down the plughole. Look into my eyes: a broken blood vessel.

My face, woman's face, tired face. Eye drops, gargle, deodorant. Pull on dirty clothes. Comb sore hands through my hair. Pinch my cheeks. Smile at myself, a mask of normal.

Mum again. The sound of toast. Smell of it burned.

'Don't worry, love, just butter it – I like the black bits.'

3

'D NEVER REALLY IMAGINED BEING PREGNANT. I'D LOOKED AT
pregnant women being given seats on buses and thought,
that's not me. I'm not like them.

Then I was – not like them but pregnant.

To start with, their father was excited by what he then
called my 'fiery side', but he wasn't sure I should be
anybody's mother. A couple of times he said he wanted to
have me locked up. I could see it hurt him to say it, but I
could also see that he meant it. He did lock me in his
bathroom once, for a whole night. I bit chunks out of my
arm. I have scars.

We cried the next day. He wrapped my arm in a
bandage he bought at the chemist – he told the lady
behind the counter that I'd burned myself frying real
chips: the kind of thing good women do, not chips from
a packet, not frozen ones, real ones, peeled and chopped
and given care. Only good women make real chips. He
said it so the woman in the chemist would think – poor
woman, burning herself making her husband such good

food, instead of her judging me for biting holes out of myself or him for being with someone like me. He wrapped the bandage carefully, making sure it wasn't loose or tight. We cuddled and the cuddle turned to sex. During the sex, blood from my arm leaked through the bandage onto the sheets. He got angry and said he couldn't live like this. But, at the time, he thought he couldn't live without me either. But people always can, really, live without each other, and in the end he did.

But back then, before he went, I decided I would have our baby. Not wise about it, just a feeling. Just an instinct. And he wrote me a poem using the letters from my name as the start of each sentence; in the poem he said he loved me like a crazy man.

I sometimes sedate myself, sometimes sleeping pills, sometimes pills meant for allergies that they advise you not use heavy machinery while taking, and then I crawl around the place half awake, wanting to bite and harm, but unable to.

Without them I am only one intention, only one feeling. The smashing, the ripping, the tearing and the screaming. No remembering of love, no deep breathing – in for four out for six, no mindfully observing my thoughts, no gratitude lists or happy-baby yoga pose, just the rushing in of something too full, too furious. The need to tear hearts out with my teeth. I am just that feeling. Just that furnace. Just a dark and foaming wilfully crashing wave that needs to crush and smash and drown. The house obliterated, furniture dragged and floating, broken wood, torn curtains, nothing to hold on to, no lifeboat coming. Destruction.

The pills at least sedate a little. I can feel the fire in my chest, like thunder far away, rumbling and capable of great harm but not overhead.

Of course, I hurt myself. I rip holes in my knees and claw at my face. I lose teeth by chewing on wood and metal. I have scars. I said I did. It's how I don't harm others as much as I could and have. It's been this way since I was a young woman. It was a thing handed down to me, the way other families might give jewellery.

But when I was pregnant, I couldn't take the pills. They might harm the baby. So their dad took me to a place in the middle of nowhere on a cliff. He locked himself in his car and watched as, blind to beauty, flaming with the need to destroy, I killed sheep and ate them, ripped the heads off rabbits. He watched as I caught a kingfisher mid-flight and tore it in half.

The day before, when I was calm and swimming in a nearby river, riding the current like it was an escalator and feeling our baby moving in my tummy like a fat snake, I'd seen the kingfisher diving right next to me. At dinner that evening I'd described it to him over and over – 'Blue, a blue dart, like a speeding gas-fire spark . . . beautiful.' He said it broke his heart to see me destroy something that had made me so happy. He pleaded with me to change.

Didn't understand how I could be so destructive.

Didn't understand how I couldn't stop myself.

Because I couldn't take the drugs while I was pregnant, we did this a few times. In the mornings he would wash my feet and scrub the blood from beneath my nails. He loved me then.

But each time, he loved me less.

And by the end – by the day our child was born – he could hardly look at me and he only loved our baby.

4

'MUM, I NEED TO GO.'

Honey and hard butter over charcoal-dusty bread. My throat is raw and the toast grazes all the way down. I grab my keys.

There's a body part on our doorstep. A small pink severed toe lying in a halo of its own blood.

With the tip of my trainer I kick it into a pile of dry leaves. It lands like a baby thrown onto a bed. I kick some more leaves over it. You can still see it, so I lean down and place one big leaf on top of it, like a crisp orange duvet.

The blood has left a little trail, a skid of it on the grey concrete. I hold out my hand to them. 'Give us your water bottle.'

They rummage in their bag, taking their time, hand it to me. 'I'll be late Mum. What are you doing?'

'Just wait!' I pour the water over the blood. It dilutes and flows away, a puddle of pink that disappears into the ground. Worm food.

I hand them back their bottle. 'There was something on the floor. Fill it up again when you get to school.'

'I know. I'm not an idiot.'

We start to walk.

'What's school today?'

They shrug. Their mouth pursed. Bum-hole lips.

'Anything good?' I push into their silence.

'School's school, Mum. It's boring.'

We walk for a while, the quiet scratching at us. They want me here; they hate me here.

'How are your friends?'

'Dunno, how are yours?'

'Don't be mean, I have friends.' I do have friends, but there are barriers, things that separate me from others.

They know this.

We walk. We might have to leave town. Might have to start again, again. We've done it before, and before that. I hate disrupting their life. And yet I do. And yet I have. And yet I will.

'You OK, Mum?' They glance at me, the start of something bolder.

'Why?' I stall, hanging back from the subject.

'I don't know. Just asking.' They stop walking and look at me. 'You seem weird.' They turn away. 'I can walk myself from here.'

And with that they up their pace and stride away from me.

5

I WATCH OTHER MUMS. ALWAYS. I WATCH THEM IN SHOPS AND on buses, in changing rooms and in doctors' waiting rooms. I watch them with their children. I watch them chatting to each other. I don't often make friends with them.

Before they were old enough to walk home from school by themselves, in the days when I had to wait for them at the gates, I'd try talking to them. Tried to join in. To fit in. But it nearly always felt scary, as if I was about to be found out. So mainly I keep my distance.

There was one once, though, another mum, who seemed more like me. I thought I saw blood under her fingernails. We talked at the gates one day and it felt different.

Our children got on. Seemed at ease in each other's company.

I asked if she thought her child would like to come back to our flat after school one day and she said yes. The kids played a computer game together and laughed. When she came to collect them, I thought maybe I could have told her things and she would have understood. I thought maybe she had things she wanted to tell me too.

Then, a few days later, they were gone, the child no longer at the school, the mum no longer waiting at the gates.

They just left town.

6

I WATCH THEM DISAPPEARING DOWN THE ROAD, TENSION IN THEIR shoulders, head dropped. They turn and look for me. See I haven't moved. Flick their hand at me as if to say, 'Go.'

I stick my fingers up at them, a V sign not the peace sign. They wrestle with a smile. Manage to subdue it. Stick their middle finger back up at me. Watch for my reaction. I clutch my chest, as if a bullet has hit me.

They mouth, 'GO AWAY.'

I shout, out loud, 'I love you.'

They flinch. I can feel the anger flying down the road, like a rock aimed at my head. They turn and keep walking. They join up with another kid their age and they walk side by side. Then another joins.

A skein of moody geese.

I stand and watch till they're out of view.

Then I start to walk home, past the park. Park being a grand word for a small patch of scruffy town green surrounded by black iron railings, the kind you might chain yourself to when you want to make a point or rip your trousers on trying to escape from something. Paint flaking, old rusting bike locks and the odd entire wheel hanging, left years ago, forgotten. The grass smells damp like old mud and it's polka-dotted with various-sized clods of dog shit at different stages of decay.

Up ahead, a small watching crowd, the blue spinning light of a parked police van flashes beams across the tree trunks, orange plastic tape tied from one to another, cordoning off a patch of balding ground. On it a body bag.

A policeman sees me, his face red with being out in the cold for longer than he'd wanted. 'Madam, keep moving.'

'What happened?' A flash of an image, teeth bite down, a tug, arm ripped from its socket, like a prawn sucked from its shell; salt blood fills my mouth, warm, still pulsing.

'Not good things, madam. Keep moving.'

I don't move. The policeman is too cold to argue. He claps his hands together for warmth, scaring a pigeon, and goes to tell a woman walking towards us with her ageing sausage-shaped terrier that she needs to take another route. The woman is dressed for a mountain. Head to toe in wet-weather gear but with crappy shoes made for the city. Flimsy scuffed black ballet pumps. Stupid outfit. Stupid woman. The small, overstuffed dog plods at her heels, sniffing for yesterday's chicken bones.

'Madam, I need you and your dog to take a detour.'

'Why? What's happened?'

'Not good things, madam.' It's a line. He's said it too much, lost its meaning.

'My dog needs a proper walk.' Caught up in herself. A body is missing a toe. 'I can't just walk her in circles. This isn't a big park.'

'Madam . . .'

'Is that a body bag?'

'Madam, please.'

But her dog has forgotten the chicken and is bristling alert, letting out a blast of sharp repetitive barks, one after the other, like an idiot on his car horn.

'Control your dog, please, madam.'

The woman tries, tugging it by the lead towards her, shouting at it to stop. But it doesn't. Instead, the barking gets faster. The dog straining on its lead, the woman's knuckles turning white as the blood leaves her fingers, the little dog growling, spitting urgent with fear.

'Madam. Control your dog!'

'I'm trying. She isn't normally like this. Silly thing, what are you doing? Stop!'

But the dog won't stop. A line of fur standing on end along its tiny angry spine, barking mad, staring, eyes fixed, towards the railing, straight at me.

It lunges, its lead the only thing holding it back, scrabbling at the ground with its claws, teeth bared, gums red, spittle on its hairy chin. I watch the owner's rising panic. I stare right back at the dog. Kneel to talk to it.

Both the woman and policeman stare at me – me, the tired middle-aged woman with the day-old clothes, and the child who's starting to hate her. I talk gently through the railing to the terrified dog, looking straight into its eyes.

'Hey, hey, silly, what's all this about? You scared? You spooked, little girl?' There's blood under my fingernails but they don't look closely enough to see.

Then quietly – you couldn't have heard, but the dog

does – I growl, a long, low animal sound, and with that the dog whimpers and retreats to its owner, curls itself around her ankles and goes silent.

The owner bends down to comfort it. 'My love, my angel, what happened? She's shaking.'

She glances between us, wanting an answer. I shrug.

'I'll leave you two ladies to it.' The policeman walks away.

Over on the grass a crowd of joggers and dog-walkers stand gripped. This is better than television.

Plastic-wrapped shape of a person rolled towards the exit. A body is missing a toe.

7

IN BETWEEN THE DAMAGE THERE IS AN US.

Not perfect, I make mistakes. I get grumpy and overtired; I snap at them when they don't deserve it. I'm no good at helping with homework, my own education was a mess. I left school early – parents too distracted with demons to recite times tables. So my knowledge is bitty and I don't know how to study. They know I can't really help them and when I try to they get irritated with me because it's fake and forced and inconsistent.

I joke about this to try to make it acceptable. 'I've been very consistent with my inconsistence.' So, there are jokes and there are days when nothing bad happens, when we talk about the kinds of food we really like, or watch crap telly, make shapes in sand with sticks, sleep late, bicker about laundry, make plans.

Their dad was around for a few years, and other men who came and went as quickly.

Two is a tiny family.

So much feeling for both to carry.

But it is an us.

8

WATCH THE WOMAN WITH HER DOG LEAVING THE PARK. SHE'S carrying it now, cradled in her arms like a baby, its muddy paws dangling, its stubby legs scrabbling, leaving dirt marks all down her jacket. She's walking purposefully but keeps glancing back at me.

On the other side of the road there's a parked ambulance, the light on its roof silently spinning, spitting blue light into the grey sky. Two paramedics leaning against the back doors.

The woman walks over to them and asks something. I watch, she glances towards me again. One of the paramedics follows her glance and looks over.

I walk away.

9

WHEN I BREASTFED THEM I GOT AN INFECTION BECAUSE they used to chew rather than suck and my nipples got so sore that they had red-raw scabs on them that wouldn't heal, like barnacles on the bottom of a boat. I called a number that was listed as being there to help women having trouble breastfeeding. It had 'League' in its title, like they might be superheroes.

A woman answered; she sounded irritated as if I had interrupted her. I told her that my baby was hungry but I had scabs on my nipples, that I'd tried a bottle but they didn't take to it and I was desperate and didn't know what to do. As I was explaining I started to cry and she coughed loudly and called me 'dear' in a not very kind way and told me to go to a sink, clean up my face and then get my baby. To grit my teeth and feed them through the pain.

She told me in a voice full of certainty that my child was the only one who mattered. She said, 'You are a mum now; you should know this.'

My milk had blood in it. Their sick had blood in it.

Their poo had little bits of dried scab in it. Feeding them was like putting my breast into a naked flame and keeping it there.

I was a mum now. I should know this.

10

AT HOME, I PUT ON THE RADIO AND RUN A BATH. I LEAVE ALL the lights off.

I'm freelance, make my own work, can't do it any other way. Not easily employed. So, I'm an 'artist' – the word makes me want to vomit. Doesn't fit with what I think of myself. It's not 'a calling', not 'my purpose', hardly a 'pleasure', it's just what I can earn some money from doing. I paint bland landscapes of trees and hills that sell well in the kind of shops that also sell hearts made of wood and tea-towels with writing on that tell you how to live: 'Always leave a little sunshine'; 'If at first you don't succeed dry again.'

I always add a tiny black cloud hidden in the perfect blue skies of my paintings that only I could notice, or you might if you have an eye for black clouds.

And their father sends us money.

I'm ashamed about it.

He's angry.

But he's not ungenerous. He loves his child and the

money is a way of demonstrating that. And I need it. I'm not self-sufficient. Too many years being something else. Each month it thuds into my account like meat slapped down on a butcher's counter. 'There you go, love. Shall I cut the fat off?'

Money hangs between the words in every conversation we have, even if it's not mentioned. It wraps itself around us like an old rusting chain.

And sometimes I wonder if, right at the bottom of it, hidden under the responsibility and care for his child, there is a tiny shard, some smudge, a stain, of leftover care for me, now faded nearly to gone but hiding there, quiet, unspoken, between cold pounds and pennies.

But mainly it feels like, no matter how much time I put in, the money just proves he is better than me, even if I provide for us in ways that can't be carried in a wallet.

My child knows he gives me money. It seems to hurt them. Like they know it's paying for more than just food and clothes, like it's also buying their father's right not to be blamed. Not to be fully seen. Not to be around. So sometimes when their father calls to speak to them they shake their head and I have to say they're busy, and their father sounds resigned.

I lower myself into the water. The heat stings the cuts. My knees have black dirt ingrained in them, a pattern like a mountain range.

There's a pain in my mouth. I push my finger in to search around: at the back a wobbly tooth. I push it. It bends away from the gum like a falling building. Plop, it tumbles into the bath and slides along the bottom in a cloud of bloody pink.

On the radio a woman is talking to another woman about feminism. We need more of it, they both agree.

Today I will tidy. Make everything like new again, even though it can never be.

My child's bedroom is a mess. Their clothes abandoned on the floor, a growing carpet of old socks, crumpled T-shirts, worn pants, stained tissues, bowls thick with dried sickly sweet cereal. Anger rises. I want to shout at them, tear at their skin for not caring about the things I do for them.

The overhead light in their room is a moon, with craters and accurate contours. Very realistic. We found it in a secondhand shop. They wanted it straight away. I'd sold an art thing recently, so I had some spare money. We had to get a man in to put it up, it's heavy and needs a chain to secure it to the ceiling. We sat and watched as the man drilled the holes, dust raining down on us all like ash. This is a rented flat, we shouldn't really drill, but I wanted my child to have their own moon.

If we leave in a rush, I will take the moon with us. I will carry it under my arm like a severed head.

I stand and turn it on. It doesn't give off much light, so it doesn't hurt my eyes. The shape of their body is embossed on the mattress. I sit and trace the outline with a finger. I pull my knees to my chest and curl up into their shape.

The shame and the grief for how I wish I had been makes me forget things. I get to the end of a day and delete. I have flashes of memories from our past but so much of their childhood and us together is gone. I ache for the memories to come back so I can hold onto our life, and maybe find parts to remind me that I haven't done all of it wrong, but it's dangerous to remember because with good memories come the bad and the bad cut into me. 'You do not deserve to breathe.'

And there I am, hurting fresh all over again. So I delete the day. And hope tomorrow I will do better.

But I do remember this: we flew once.

Our feet dangled above the world and the air took our breath away. I had my arms round their waist, I could smell the suntan cream on the back of their neck, see them watching everything, looking down on the world like it could never hurt them.

I fall asleep. When I wake up my phone is ringing. It takes me a moment to realize it's real, not a dream. Sometimes in my dreams my mum calls me, or I bump into her at the supermarket, and she says things like 'Watch it,' then evaporates.

I answer quickly and then instantly wish I hadn't because my voice has cracks in it and I don't sound the way a mum should at this time of the day. 'Yes?'

'Mum?'

'Yes, love, are you OK? Where are you?'

'They're asking all the parents to come to the school. You need to come. They're saying we can't walk home by ourselves.'

In the background I can hear echoey school corridors, voices, alarm in them.

'Mum? Did you hear me? We're all in the hall, they need you to come.'

'I heard you. I'll come. I'm coming.'

Their voice goes quieter. Like they don't want someone to hear. 'A boy . . . Mum. A boy from our school is missing.'

A pause.

'I'm coming, love, hold on.'

THEY WALKED EARLY, BEFORE THEY COULD TALK.

After a day of crawling, they started pulling themselves up on anything they could reach, chair legs, my shins, the walls. Straightening their tiny chubby legs like unfolding tiny tree trunks, then fearlessly letting go of whatever it was they were holding on to, wobbling triumphant into a moment of standing, before losing their balance and flopping back down onto their nappy-padded bum, then doing it over and over again.

I was sitting on the sofa. I'd left them in the kitchen, just down the hall where I could hear them but could also create some space between us. I wasn't good at being just the two of us together, face-to-face, for as long as parenting a toddler asks of you. I had to get away, sit alone, to stare for a moment into how much I hated myself for not being able to do it all, how much their need for me made me feel both humbled and desperate.

I was sitting with my head in my hands, trying to believe I was a capable woman, when there was a small thump, then another, then a loud gurgle as if they were trying to call to me but didn't yet know any of the words they should use.

I jumped up, fearful of what might have happened and angry they couldn't leave me alone for just a few minutes more – and there they were. Naked apart from the heavy lopsided yellowing nappy clinging round their waist, their bare feet arched like tense fists, toes gripping the carpet, arms stretched out either side as if they were balancing on a wire. Their whole face electric with concentration, the pure wonder of their achievement.

One determined step at a time they teetered towards me.

I felt simultaneously overwhelmed with love and flooded with dread at the idea that they could now find me whenever they wanted to.

I knelt down and they breathlessly tottered towards me and collapsed into my arms, almost purring with pride.

Later that evening when I thought they were asleep in my bed, they walked to me again. I couldn't make them sleep in their cot, and most nights I didn't even try. The trying took too much out of both of us, so I just gave in, and we slept together in my bed. Wrong, I'm sure, bad habits forming nightly like mildew, weak mother, not able to set a boundary mother.

I was sitting on the landing at the top of the stairs. Their dad had come over on his way back from work to say good night to them. He didn't live with us. A few months before, I'd told him to leave. I'd said it in a rage. He'd gone and he'd stayed away. We both felt hard done by. We both blamed the other.

I'd stood outside the bedroom listening to him singing our child a song about pigs and toes and reading to them about happy endings and farts. But when he came out of the room the gentleness faded and we'd got into a fight. The same old 'This is your fault', round and round, over and over.

He was standing at the bottom of the stairs by the front door, half leaving but half not finished with telling me how angry I made him.

I was sitting at the top of the stairs rubbing the side of my head against the wall. I'd given up answering back and had started crying. He was shouting at me, saying that crying was manipulative, that it left no room for anyone else to feel.

Behind me I heard the pad of small bare feet on carpet – no longer sprawled asleep in my bed but awake and using their newfound skill of steps to come and find me. Out of our bedroom and down the hall, swaying with determination until they reached me and flumped down, where they turned and made a sort of pre-word grunting noise down the stairs at their father, a warning of some sort, then turning away from him and towards me, and with tiny hands outstretched, like waking petals, they pushed at my chin urging me to lift my head and with bold fingers they wiped under my eyes making a repeated sound, Sssh, ssssh. Ssssh, ssssssh.

WE MAY HAVE TO LEAVE AGAIN. I WILL SNATCH THEM FROM friendships, teachers they like and who like them, and the home with the moon on a chain and the shapes of our bodies still forming on the mattresses.

I'll tear us away. Tear up what we've made. Destroy repair, destroy repair. Make new, make new, make new.

I go to the bathroom, scream at my face in the mirror. Bite a mouth-sized chunk out of my upper arm, spit the stringy wet flesh down the loo and flush it. Press a towel over the wound until it stops pulsing blood, bandage it with gauze and plasters.

Make their bed, put a wash on, shove the blood-soaked towel into a black bin liner along with my piss-stained nightie and chuck them into the rubbish.

Check the fridge, make a note to buy pasta and Nutella, get my coat, smile at myself in the mirror, tell myself to fuck off, then leave the house.

When I arrive at the school, two teachers are minding the gate, stamping their feet against the cold, breathing foggy plumes of iced air as they chat quietly to each other, nodding earnest smiles at anyone who passes.

Everyone is talking quietly. No shouting. No ball being kicked against the wall, no bell, no trample of feet eager to get home, no screaming laughs, no shouting taunts, no mums chatting shit and moaning about their loft extensions taking too long, no car horns honking to say, 'Over here!' The place has the air of a hospital ward, or a cemetery.

Kids come out with their parents, who nod pained goodbyes at the two teachers and scuttle off shrouded in concern and each other.

I make my way to the hall. An urge to scrape my fingernails along the walls. I push open the heavy, weighted doors. Sound turns to echo.

A large old TV on wheels blathers in the corner, burbling a cartoon, kids sitting round it on low orange chairs, one eye on the screen, the other on the phones resting in their laps, like illuminated newborns.

Teachers standing in huddles, more whispering, lowered heads.

I see them before they see me. They're not watching the cartoon, they're sitting on the waxed wooden steps leading up to the stage, their back to me, talking to someone.

I walk over. I want to call out but am sure calling out would be seen as wrong – try to gauge what is considered right.

About a foot from them I say their name. 'Hey, love, I'm here.'

They turn. They're talking to another child.

A girl, I decide.

Sitting on the stage, huddled in a black overcoat. Short hair, black makeup around her eyes, the kind that says 'Be careful' rather than 'Come in'. She looks like she's been crying. She wipes her nose on her hand.

'Hey, hi, I'm here,' I interrupt.

'Yeah, I can see that.'

'Should we go?' I ask, unsure of what is needed of me.

'Yep.' They don't move.

'How about your friend?' I step forward. 'Are your parents coming?' I ask, holding my hand out for the girl to shake but, fast, my child slaps it away.

'Mum! What are you doing? Quite weird!'

I can feel my face going red. I step back. 'I'm just checking, love, if your friend needs help getting home.'

'She's OK,' they snap.

Yes, a girl.

The girl stands. 'My dad's coming. Thanks.'

13

AT FIRST, THEIR DAD CAME OFTEN TO SAY GOODNIGHT. THEN that stopped and he'd come and take them to stay with him on weekends, not consistent but not never. Sometimes they'd go to their dad's mother's.

She lived a drive away in a bungalow by the sea. Her husband had died years ago, and she was angry at the world for letting it happen. But it was a heart attack, nobody's fault, just a body failing. Her home always felt damp and cold, even in summer. There were no severed toes on the doorstep, but it had a pain of its own. A musty low-grade unhappiness.

Their dad would come and get them on a Friday night, unable to make eye contact with me; he'd wait in our kitchen while our child gathered up their stuff. I'd ask how his mum was.

'Fine,' he'd say, keen not to engage.

And then I'd ask how he was.

'Fine,' he'd answer, cold. 'You nearly ready?' he'd call past me. 'We need to go.'

He would never ask how I was.

I'd leave him standing in our kitchen all stiff and uncomfortable like even the room I lived in disgusted him in some way, and I'd go into the bedroom and help our child pack, tell them to have a great time, and they'd look at me, letting me know that was asking too much, reminding me – this was about adults handing their child around like luggage, not about great times.

On more than one occasion they asked if they had to go, said they didn't feel like anyone really wanted them there. They'd rather take their chances with me than feel tolerated by their dad's family.

But I thought they should be with their dad whenever possible. I felt that was what a normal broken family would aim for. So, I'd convince them to go and, being the generous soul they have always been, they did.

Sometimes they came home happy and told me good stories about things they'd done, sometimes they came home quiet and wouldn't tell me anything.

Sometimes, while they were away, I met up with men. Usually it ended badly. Sometimes I hurt someone or myself, and if that happened, I would worry that the flat smelt of blood, which I didn't want for when they came back, so I'd spend the Sunday scrubbing everything, making it nice and lighting candles. Sometimes I just curled up in a ball and slept the whole weekend, only waking up to have a bath and make some food when I knew they were on their way home.

But in the last few years their dad has been in touch less and less. He said he didn't think I should force our child to see him. He said he felt like they didn't really enjoy seeing him. I tried to explain that I thought children that age didn't really want to be with either of their parents but that we should still make the effort to let them know we wanted to be with them. He said he'd text our child and ask what they felt like doing. I said I thought a parent asking their child if they wanted to see them or not was maybe sending confusing messages. Then there would be a silence, which I knew was intended for me to consider how unacceptable it was *me* lecturing anyone about confusing parenting.

Sometimes I ask them, as casually as I can sound, 'Have you heard from your dad?'

Usually they answer, with a shutdown shrug, 'No.'

Then I feel bad for asking. Like I've been cruel, high-lighted the lack.

Most of the time I feel it's my fault that they don't see each other very much. That he is punishing our child with his absence because of things I have done. Like if I were a totally different woman, whole other things would have been possible.

But very occasionally another thought occurs, about how their dad could have tried harder to stay or could have helped me to manage things better, could have focused on what was good about me, and then it may have flourished and grown stronger, like when you give a plant more light or special soil. But that type of thought doesn't last long.

14

THERE HAS BEEN A LONG GAP WHEN NEITHER OF US HAS SPOKEN. They are sitting at the table, folded double in an angry brace position, armadillo-hunch back. No entry. Ignoring a Nutella sandwich, their head buried in folded arms, fingers clenched into boiling white-hot fists.

I'm standing, leaning on the kitchen counter. Urge to breathe fire, to tear skin. But instead, 'You seem really angry. Are you angry with me? I'm sorry.'

I use that word too much. I know it makes them cross. Sorry for what? The past? Now? Who I am? What's to come? A man once said to me I should have 'Sorry' tattooed across my forehead so I didn't have to say it any more and instead could just lift my hair and show it when needed. I say it anyway.

They don't reply. Instead they flinch, making sure I see, muscles tightening when I speak. 'My love. You know if I could change things I would. I wouldn't be me, which I know would be so much better, but then you also wouldn't be you.'

We've gone down this road of thinking so many times before – if I had been born a different person, if I'd made better choices, hadn't met their dad, had decided I wasn't the kind of woman who should have a baby, it always ends up with both of us not existing. So, the conversation has to turn to seeing silver linings and what is good about me being me and them being my child.

When they were younger, they accepted those interpretations, went along with the narrative. They were a child desperate to stay connected to a parent, justifiably afraid of what their mother was capable of, but just as afraid of losing her. They were my ally, my companion, me and them, against the world.

Now the knot is loosening. I can see the thoughts growing, their own perception becoming the truth, bubbling into being, like those sea creatures that live right down deep, in the dark, and don't even know about sky, suddenly coming to the surface and seeing light, newly growing sight.

Ready for change. Ready for air.

Maybe they don't need me, maybe life without me would be better. Maybe my silver linings are ash. What doesn't kill you doesn't make you stronger and is perfectly capable of still killing you. Those fabricated silver linings I try to convince us of simply honey-smoothing mum-talk, parental coercion, created to guide them back to me, over and over, to turn away from their own feelings and towards mine.

Not to be angry with me.

So, name it, I tell myself. Say out loud all you have done wrong; prove to them you know how bad you are. 'You're angry with me, that's OK, that makes sense. I understand. I've made terrible mistakes.'

The muscles in their fists clench tighter as if the skin might split open like a sausage filling with heat. The more I tell them I understand, tell them they have a right to their anger, the more I am blocking their path, controlling their flames, telling them where to burn and what to set alight. And reminding them always, and most importantly, not to set light to me.

They mutter into the crook of their elbow. Low, almost so I can't hear, but enough that I do. 'I fucking hate you.'

'Love.' I lean towards them . . . I could rip their head off now. Don't they know how hard it is? 'My love.'

They look up at me, yellow flecks in their eyes – I have those – and they stand so they are facing me.

15

I WAS HAPPY THE DAY THEY FOUND OUT FATHER CHRISTMAS didn't exist.

It was a couple of years ago. A boy at school had gone around telling all the other kids that Father Christmas was just a made-up story. 'He doesn't exist. It's just your parents.'

My child had corrected the boy straight away, they told me later. 'What if you don't have parents? What if you just have one parent?'

'Then it's just them. It's your mum or whatever. It's all shit. He's not a real thing. And if you think it is, then you're an idiot.'

I remember the look on their face when they came home. Our tree was up, stocking hanging at the end of their bed. Two is a small number to fill a Christmas so I always tried hard to make it right, even though I couldn't always control what happened and sometimes it went very wrong.

They walked in the door, eyes squinting, looking straight at me, examining me, as if they'd caught me mid-crime.

I asked how their day was. They ignored the question,

dumped their bag on the floor, walked to the table, pulled back a chair and sat, arms folded, as if ready to interview someone who was well known for lying.

'Who is Father Christmas?' The question flew towards me like a javelin.

To be the child of a mum like me is to have the expected safety and comfort of childhood poked and prodded and sometimes quite simply ripped away from you. So when we could we'd cling at its edges, the way you do when someone you share the bed with is stealing all the blanket and you have to hold on tight or feel the cold.

If I answered this question truthfully another huge part of their childhood would be over, ruined, never to be retrieved.

I'd been a good Father Christmas.

I'd made reindeer-hoof prints over our carpet by holding three fingers in the shape I imagine reindeer toes look from underneath, licking my fingers and then dipping them in talcum powder for snow and dabbing them all the way through the flat. I'd nibbled the carrot in a convincing reindeer-bite way, I'd written notes of thanks from him and his mouse. (In our home he had a mouse with him.)

I'd waited up late into the night to make sure they were properly asleep before I filled the stocking, my eyes drifting shut and my body aching for rest. And I'd always remembered that Father Christmas's wrapping paper must be different from the paper parents use, and I'd nearly ripped their father's throat out when he turned up one Christmas Eve to drop off his contribution to presents, with both his and the ones from 'Father Christmas' wrapped in the same paper.

'You can't fucking do that! Father Christmas doesn't have the same paper as us!' I hissed at him while our child's back was turned.

I remember he shrugged at me with the disdain he often had when talking to me, as if just being who I was meant he didn't have to listen to a word I said, even when I was right.

I remember how I saw the start of the question they were now hurling at me beginning to form when they woke the next morning and noticed straight away that their dad and Father Christmas had used the same wrapping paper. But they weren't ready for the undoing of it all: they wanted a story to hold on to so I made one up about how Father Christmas and normal fathers often did the same things – like it was a 'father' sort of thing – which I could tell they weren't quite sure about but decided to swallow, the way you do a vegetable you hate the taste of but have been told is healthy. I hated myself for my stupid story as it made dads 'closer' to Father Christmas just because they hadn't bothered to think ahead or predict disappointment, and it left mums out altogether and it came to me way too easily without question.

I also hated myself because I couldn't bring myself to rewrap his presents. A part of me – the bleeding wounded part – must have wanted my child to notice how shit their dad was being compared to me, even if it meant blowing apart their innocence and joy. I was prepared to hurt them to be acknowledged.

'Mum, who is Father Christmas? It's you, isn't it? You better tell me; I'll get bullied if you lie to me.'

My child has chewed on and swallowed so many truths:

your mother is capable of terrible things and sometimes your safety is the last thing on her mind; your granny is dead – she chose to die; your dad sends money instead of time and now he hardly calls; we don't have a home that we will always stay in, like those other kids – sometimes we just have to up in the night, move and start all over again. They've chewed and they've swallowed, and they still manage to be kind and to tell me they love me, and to say, 'It's OK,' and 'I don't mind' and to genuinely laugh at my jokes.

They've faced a lot of truth. And now they were asking for more. 'Mum, I'm not a baby. Tell me. Is it you?'

But there was something in the heart of this truth that I did want them to know. Yes, I can rip heads clean off necks with my bare teeth and at times I have to sedate myself so that I don't. Yes, I wear my guilt like a blood-soaked cape, and I beg of you a forgiveness that I have no right to ask for. Yes, you have scars that were caused by me. Yes, you have every right to hate me, and when you grow up you have every right to move far, far away, to never speak to me again and to say 'I don't talk about her' when people ask about your mother. All those things are true, but this is true too: it was me, all the time, all the years. That was me.

I am the bad woman, I am the bad mother, but I am also that man. I am Father Christmas.

'Mum. Is it you?'

I answered. Yes.

They said nothing, just nodded, stood and walked into their bedroom and shut the door. The flat went silent, the air full of another undoable moment.

I sat on the floor, curled my knees up to my chest and bit into the fat of my palm until my mouth filled with blood and my teeth scraped the bone.

About an hour went past. Then the door opened, and they came out and asked what we were having to eat. I stood, surprised by their composure and the lightness in their voice. They saw the blood on my hand, went to the sink, wet some kitchen towel, came back to me, told me to stand up and held the damp tissue to the wound. 'You shouldn't do this to yourself,' they said.

Then they walked away, chucked the bloodied tissue in the bin and asked again, 'What are we eating?'

'Baked potatoes?'

'Cool,' they said. 'Call me when they're done.' And with that they went back into their room shutting the door behind them again.

I made dinner, all the time preparing myself for the tears and the pain they would inevitably have to express. When the food was cooked, I knocked on their door and called to them, 'It's ready, love.'

They came out, and as I was getting the potatoes out of the oven they asked if they could help. This wasn't totally usual.

'I'll set the table, Mum,' they said, already getting knives and forks from the drawer. Once they had done that they asked if I needed them to grate cheese.

'Wow,' I said. 'OK, yes, please, but mind your fingers.'

I watched as they grated. Something new, something changed. 'You OK?' I asked.

They stopped grating, lumped a big pile of cheese onto a nearby plate and put it on the table. 'I'm fine,' they answered, plonking themselves down in a chair and patting the one next to them, gesturing for me to sit too. 'You should eat, Mum,' they said, forking a potato onto the plate laid for me.

I sat. Said thanks and stared at them. They caught me staring.

'I think I knew he didn't exist. I've known for a while, I think, like since a few years ago probably.'

'Really?'

'Yeah, that year Dad used the same wrapping paper. I kind of guessed then, but you seemed like you really needed me to not know so I didn't say anything.'

'Really?'

'Yeah, I mean of course I wasn't sure, but like I did sort of know.'

'And how do you feel now?' I don't always ask my child this question, in case I can't bear to hear their answer, but this time I did. Just straight like that: 'How do you feel now?'

'You did a lot,' they said. 'You did it all, for years. Reindeer paw prints and all that stuff. It's pretty impressive, Mum. Thank you.'

They pushed the cheese towards me.

'You're welcome,' I said, filling with a feeling I rarely allow myself to have.

16

'I FUCKING HATE YOU!'

I can see they've scared themselves. Scarred themselves.

I long to bite back, can feel nails growing in my finger beds, sharp and cruel. I dig them into my palm. I try to sound like only love sounds, try to ignore what shame feels like, what anger feels like, what not feeling like a good enough mum, what feeling like a very bad one, feels like. 'OK, I hear you – you hate me.'

'Don't just say shit back at me like they say you should in one of your stupid books – How to Be a Better Person – or some shit like that.'

My voice catches fire, a flash of a flame. 'Oi, that's mean. At least I try. You could have a parent who doesn't even read the books.'

'OR I could have a parent who doesn't even *need* to read the fucking books. I could have a parent who just fucking *is* a better fucking person.' They wince each time they say 'fuck'. Like it's hurting them, but they can't stop. They want there to be hurt.

'OK! That's enough with the swearing.'

'Fuck off – you swear.'

'Don't talk to me like that.'

'Fuck you! I want to leave! I don't want to be here with you.'

There's blood filling my hand – my nails are reaching bone. My chest shudders. The sobs come. I don't want to cry; I know the sobs will upset them.

They can't hate me when I cry. Or they can hate me, but they can't leave me. They have to care. They always have. A child is not meant to do the caring. A mother is not meant to need it. And yet always we have ebbed and flowed, swapped roles and swapped back again. It's not right. But it's us. And I carry the shame for it, like they will carry the scars and rage the way I did with my mother.

So the tears come and I can't stop them. I open my palm. They look down. Blood drips onto the floor. I fold down into a crushed paper bag of a mum.

'I'm so sorry. I'm so sorry. You have every right to hate me. I hate myself.'

I fold my bloodstained fingers into a fist and aim it at my face.

'Mum! Don't . . . Mum.'

I land a blow. A cheekbone so used to me hitting it it's made of splinters and old bruises.

'Mum, stop . . . stop. I don't hate you.' They kneel down, clumsy, voice choked. 'Don't hurt yourself.'

They take my hand, their hand no longer tiny – now bigger than mine – and open my fingers. Holes in my palm where my nails dug in. 'It's not fair on us when you hurt yourself, Mum. You shouldn't do it.'

I push my head into the wall behind me. Breathe deep. 'You'd be better off without me.'

They flinch at the self-pity and threat. 'Don't say that stuff, Mum.'

'A child shouldn't have to help their mum.'

They go to tell me that they don't mind; I go to tell them that they should.

But then – unusual – our doorbell rings. One short sharp buzz, then a longer, more insistent one.

A boy is missing and a foot is missing its toe and – somebody is at our door.

17

WHEN MY BACK IS SO SORE THAT I CAN'T REACH MY TOES, my child has helped me to clean blood from between them.

Once I thanked them with a trip to the seaside. I phoned their school and said they were sick. We got the train, ate salmon sandwiches and drank a thick yellow juice with bananas in it that felt like snot but tasted better.

We walked along the sea front. It was October. Not summer season. Arcades empty. Grey-black sea and constant pin-sharp spits of rain.

About twenty minutes out of town there's a very old sea pool. When the tide's in, it's immersed and you wouldn't know it was there, but when the tide goes out, suddenly a seawater swimming pool appears, bigger than any pool you'd find in a city and surrounded by seaweed and barnacle-covered walls. Flat as a pancake inside while the waves lap at the edges, knocking at the walls, waiting to be allowed back in. We walked to it from the station, through the rain, collars up, shoulders hunched.

There was nobody else there, just seagulls and the odd

jet-black cormorant diving for fish. We changed on the beach and giggled about how cold it was. I laid my coat on the damp hard sand and we stood on it to keep our feet warm until the moment we were ready to run in.

I'm a good swimmer. I've made them brave about water. My mum did the same with me – no formal swimming lessons, just chuck you in and encourage you not to drown, pulling you out at the last minute if it looked like you might, then chucking you in again, knowing that at some point the instinct to survive will get you kicking.

We entered from the beach, the cold biting into our calves, then our thighs, then, before we lost our nerve, I dived under, and they followed. What choice did they have? I glanced over. They came up gasping for breath but smiling. We swam to the centre of the pool. It was big, about three normal swimming pools big. I was treading water, they were treading water. Nobody anywhere. Just the sound of our breath and the impatient waves on the wall outside.

Then, about ten feet from us, a black shape moved under the surface, and a face popped up, looked at us and disappeared back under. They screamed, then scrambled and splashed towards me.

'Mum! What is it? MUM!' They gulped in water as they grabbed on to me, their hands slipping on my shoulders like we were both made of wet soap, finally getting hold of me and gripping around my neck, trying to climb me like a tree.

I looked closer towards the place we saw the face. The water flat. Nothing. Above us seagulls laughed. Then, after a few seconds, it was up again. Grey shiny skin. Navy oval blinking empty eyes.

I pulled them close into me and held tight round their chest, feeling their panicked breath, churning in and out. 'It's OK. It's OK, my love, look . . . it's a seal. It's just a seal.'

'What if it wants to hurt us?'

I couldn't be sure, but I decided to tell them it doesn't want to. I explained to them that it must have swum in when the tide was high, and the walls weren't visible and now it's stuck and has to wait for the tide to come back in so it can go free. I said it's probably much more afraid of us than we are of it and we need to let it know that we're friendly.

They looked at me, the way children do when they are trying to work out whether to believe you. The seal popped up again. It looked like it was asking for something – it could have been reassurance.

My child whispered to it and to themselves, 'It's OK.'

The perfect pitch-black-circle eyes blinked at us. Then ducked back under. I felt my child tense again. 'Where is it? Where's it gone?'

'He's just swimming,' I said.

Their teeth started chattering while they talked. Mine too.

'He got stuck,' they whispered to me.

'Yep, he has. Shall we swim to say hello, so he knows he doesn't have to worry about us?'

I stroked a strand of wet hair out of their eyes, which were facing away from me, glued to the flat water and the place where the seal last surfaced.

They nodded bravely while asking me to promise I would swim right next to them, and I said I would. Together we waited till he popped up again, then swam towards him. Each time we got close, he blinked or winked and swam away. We played this game until our lips were blue and our skin was a mass of rigid goose bumps.

When the cold started to reach our bones, we hurried to the beach and got changed, which was difficult as our fingers were so cold it was hard to move them. I did up their zips and buttons and struggled with my own. They didn't take their eyes off the water.

Once we were dressed, I suggested we go and find hot chocolate. But my child was worried about the seal. They wanted to wait and watch the tide change so they could know that he escaped.

They were shivering hard now. Teeth chattering so much it was almost impossible to make out their words. But they were determined. I stood behind them, pushed my chest against their back, wrapped my arms tightly around them and blew warm air into their neck while they fixed their gaze on the seal as he bobbed up, watched us, went under, then bobbed up again.

Each time he did they whispered to themselves, to me, to him, 'There you are.'

Slowly the tide came in and the waves started to sneak back over the wall. After about ten minutes, the pool had disappeared. The sea spread out in front of us, wide and endless, right out to touch the edge of the sky. The pool might never have been.

'Go, go on . . . You can go now,' they called to him, their words getting caught in the wind and chucked away.

We watched together as the seal swam past the point where the wall had been and out towards the distance.

'Bye, take care – we were your friends.'

They made us wait to check he was going in the right direction and wouldn't get trapped again. Once they were satisfied that he was free, we went to find the hot chocolate.

I reminded them that they couldn't tell anybody about our day. As far as the school was concerned, they'd had a tummy bug.

They said that's fine. They told me they loved the seal. I told them they were brave.

On the train on the way back they fell asleep resting their head against my shoulder. A young woman smiled at me, moved by our relationship. I smiled back pretending for a moment that we are only ever this.

When we got home, I shouted at them for taking too long getting ready for bed.

18

THE FRIEND WITH THE WARNING EYE MAKEUP IS AT OUR DOOR.
They are suddenly very tender, grown-up, talking to her
like we are the safe place that she has run to. Their voice
is gentle and warm, signalling to her that all is well in our
home and that she was right to come.

'Mum, it's OK if she comes in for a bit, isn't it? We can
make some extra dinner, can't we?'

She stands in our doorway, her body hunched. It's been
raining, her shoulders are soaked. She keeps sniffing. 'I
don't want to be a problem.'

'You're not – she's not, is she, Mum?'

'Do your parents know you're here?' I ask.

They shoot a look at me, not the right question.

'They might be worried,' I carry on, trying to stay in charge.

'Mum, it's not simple,' right at me, their voice full of
protection – for her.

She sniffs again, then wipes her eyes. Black makeup
smudges on the back of her hands. But I notice something
else. 'My dad doesn't care.'

'I'm sure he does.'

'Mum, leave it. She can eat with us – yes?'

'OK, yes.' I saw something.

'We're going to my room,' they tell me, then their tone changes, back to the one just for her, gentle, like they're talking to a wounded thing. 'This way, my room's through here.' They lead, she follows.

I know what I saw.

Her hand, when she wiped her eyes.

Blood under her fingernails.

19

MY MUM ATTACKED ME MANY TIMES. BIT HUGE FLESHY chunks out of me.

My father was mainly present in his absence, relying on and vilifying her in equal measure.

She was as ferocious with her love for us as she was ferocious. She came to a school parents' evening once and flipped the table. The teacher said something about me being lazy, my work not being up to scratch. She compared my workbook with another child's, slapping mine down in front of Mum like a stinking dead fish, then handing her the other girl's book carefully and proud as if handing over a swaddled newborn.

'Look at the difference. This is the kind of work we expect.'

I sat next to Mum, both of us on small metal school chairs. I could hear the blood pumping in her heart. All around us, kids and their parents sat on the same stupidly small chairs opposite diligent teachers quietly burbling, polite and accepting.

'Could do better, excellent work, will try harder.'

Mum pushed the other girl's book across the table towards my teacher, not even looking at it. While she spoke she stroked the cover of mine, like it was made of soft fur.

'You should be ashamed,' she hissed, low and clear, at the teacher.

I felt terrified but excited.

The teacher started to cluck back. 'There are standards we must keep. We can't make exceptions just because a child is a bit different. They need to learn how to give what is being asked of them . . .' I could see the teacher tensing, knowing Mum wasn't going to just accept and nod politely. She kept glancing around anxiously to see who might be close enough to protect her if she needed it, her voice, all the time, getting higher and more strangled.

'Our job is to make sure our children can go out and be a part of society, not separate from it.' Then she tried to hand the other child's book back to Mum, tried to use a soft, strong tone but her fear betrayed her, and her voice started cracking.

'Please, look at this child's work. The difference is obvious. We have to help your daughter to be able to confor—'

With that Mum tilted her head backwards, mouth up to the strip-lit ceiling and yelled a noise. Not a word, a noise.

Everyone turned round, kids laughed out of nerves, parents gasped. There was a rumour that one boy shat himself. Then she stood, her metal chair clattering as it skidded backwards across the polished wooden floor, pushed me behind her, put both her hands under the tabletop and threw it into the air.

The teacher screamed. People rushed to help her. The hall was filled with noise and the clatter of table legs crashing down, but above it all, I could still hear Mum's heartbeat.

She grabbed my hand, kissed my head and marched us fast towards the double doors which led to the playground. She turned and shouted back into the chaos, 'Sheep! Fucking sheep!'

The next day, a letter arrived saying I was suspended and that the school was unsure they could allow me back, that they were seeking advice and we'd hear from them in due course.

Mum kept pills by her bed in a wooden box carved into the shape of a ship. They came in rows in small foil strips. She used them to sedate herself and occasionally me. She gave me two with some powdery chocolate milk that she hadn't stirred very well so the powder clagged in lumps on my tongue and stuck to my gums like wet cement, then she put me to bed with a hot-water bottle. I couldn't lift my head, it felt like I was at the bottom of a swimming pool and I couldn't reach anybody. I slept for a few days. When I woke up everything in our house was packed into boxes, Mum looked exhausted but tried to hide it, and Dad had gone.

20

I PUT ON SOME JAZZ. IT MAKES ME FEEL LIKE WE ARE A DIFFERENT kind of people.

I turn the lights down so the kitchen feels warm and inviting. I can hear them talking through their door. At first the friend was crying, her voice full of urgency and panic. I could tell they were doing all they could to calm her. It didn't sound easy – a few times I nearly went in: I felt worried for them dealing with her feelings on their own. Then after a while they said something in the voice I know they use to make jokes and she laughed. Then they both laughed. Since then they've been talking and laughing.

I feel excluded, jealousy growing in my chest like brambles. But I also feel glad they are in my house. That way my child hasn't gone. Maybe if I am nice to this friend, they won't want to go anywhere, ever, but I must be careful not to overdo that because it could have the opposite effect and they'll be in a hurry to get away from me.

I cook pasta and make more than we need because I

don't want to be one of those parents that makes too little and leaves everyone hungry.

We were once invited to another family's house. The father knitted their clothes, and the mother played the cello; they had exam results in frames on the wall. She fed us dry chicken legs and boiled potatoes. Tiny portions. My child finished their food quickly and reached out to take another potato, but the mother slapped their hand away and pushed the bowl towards the father. 'No more. Those are for Daddy.'

I wanted to rip her arm from its socket. To put my fist through their boasting art and then use the broken glass to slash to ribbons their smug, ugly hand-knitted sweaters.

I want this new friend in my child's room to be able to reach out and take as much pasta as she wants.

I knock gently on their door. 'It's ready, love.'

21

I DON'T REMEMBER MANY TOYS. I DON'T REMEMBER PLAYING.

I remember a doll's house, with tiny-flowered wallpaper and mini-chandeliers. I didn't know what to do with it. Mum bought me dolls to put in it and I just cut off all their hair.

I remember her being around, unhappy or working, newly in love or angry, but not playing.

When I try to remember times with Dad it's like the focus won't fix. It's forever blurred.

I don't remember what happened to the doll's house. I remember Mum cared; she wanted me to play but she didn't play with me. And I didn't play because I was too busy watching her, trying to work out when her mood would change and working out if I had any power over that.

Then years later, when my child was small, someone left another old doll's house in the street with a note on it saying, 'Take me.'

I carried it home. It was scrappy, loved and then abandoned.

I painted its walls with our leftover house paint. I stuck up some wrapping paper for wallpaper and passport photos of my child and me with tin foil round them to make frames so they looked like miniature portraits, the kind you might see in a stately home.

My child liked these small plastic figures with plastic hair that you could remove and swap around, like brown or orange or yellow helmets. They came as all sorts of things – cowboys, nurses, doctors, firemen, builders, mums, children. Also, dogs, cats, parrots, even a cavewoman with her very own club. I bought as many as I could find.

The floor of their bedroom, in front of the refurbished abandoned doll's house, was covered with them, lying there waiting to be played with. And they would sit for hours, cross-legged, lost in it, moving the figures around, making voices, making scenes, making them fight, making them kiss, putting them to sleep in tiny wooden beds that I'd laid a sheet of toilet paper over to look like a blanket.

I would sit nearby and watch as they played. Sometimes, when the closeness was too much and I felt they were disappointed in me for not being the type of mum who knew what to do, I sat in the hall outside and listened.

And sometimes, when I really couldn't bear feeling so useless, I would pay someone to play with them and I would walk the streets or bite something.

I hardly ever joined in. I didn't know how to. Didn't know how to relax enough to. Couldn't calm my mind enough to find the words, the imagination, the attention.

Then one night, after they had fallen asleep, I stayed sitting on the floor where I had been impatiently reading them a story, exhausted as my voice stumbled to sound warm and calm. I stayed on the floor next to their bed and then I noticed the doll's house. I stared at it for a while, then I crawled towards it and sat in front of it, crossed my legs and began to move the figures around, whispering their voices, making scenes.

A cowboy in the kitchen, a fireman in bed with a monkey, a ghost in a cupboard watching an old lady lying on the floor staring up at her ceiling, a mum and a child standing on the roof, a cavewoman hitting another with her very own club. For about a week, every night after my child had gone to sleep, I'd sit there on my own playing with their toys.

22

SHE DOESN'T EAT MUCH, PUSHES THE PASTA AROUND LIKE IT frightens her, the red sauce staining the plate.

They're watching her all the time, willing her to feed herself, take care of herself, stay alive. We chat a bit about school, what she enjoys, what she doesn't. They tell me how talented she is.

'She's a proper artist, Mum. Her drawing is brilliant.'

I can feel they want me to connect with her.

'Not proper, not an artist, it's not brilliant. It's OK.' She speaks like each word is a challenge to get out, like she doesn't want to be seen but with a hint of being relieved that she is.

'Believe me, Mum, it's brilliant.'

I say I do believe them. I want to shout to my child, 'Forget her being brilliant. Don't care about that. Don't give any of your care to her. Care about you, and with any spare care you have left, care for me. We have no room for this young woman and her needs and her shitty father and the blood under her nails.' But I don't say this. I bite into my lip and I nod and say I believe them.

She says she hears that I can draw, that she hears I'm really good.

I'm tempted to join her with the self-denial: 'No, no, I'm not that good, they're just saying that to bond with you. I'm not good. In so many ways I'm not good . . .' But I catch myself and decide to try not to pick at myself like a scab.

'I like drawing.' My answer neither destroys me nor raises me up. Best I can do.

'No. Mum's good. Like you.' Not like me. No, not like me please.

She's been twirling pasta round and round on her fork – there's too much on it to fit in a mouth.

She sees me looking at her. Drops her fork and hides her hands under the table. 'That was really nice pasta,' she says, her plate still half full.

'You haven't eaten much. You sure you don't need more?'

'We had crisps in my room,' they say.

There's a pause. Something is waiting to be said. But I don't know what it is.

I leave space for them to speak. But they don't. I fill it. 'It's getting late, love.'

They flinch when I call them love. Maybe they're not my love any more. Drifting, drifting, gone. Don't go. Let's run again, missing boys, toe on a doorstep, and this girl with her obvious needs that you obviously care for. Let's run, my love.

'Is your dad going to come and get you?'

'No. It's OK. I can walk.'

'I think your mum might worry if you were walking on your own . . .'

They shoot me a look. Stare hard at me.

Her jaw clenches so I hear her teeth grind. There's a small growl in her voice. 'I don't have a mum. It's just me and my dad.'

'I'm very sorry. That must be hard.'

23

MY MUM ENDED HER LIFE OUT OF CHOICE.

She'd been diagnosed with an illness that would affect her mind and she had no desire to see how it would pan out.

I was with her when she did it. Expecting big last words when only small ones came. She told us which Oxfam to take her clothes to – the one with the nicer staff. Apologized for a moment of emotion, turned to the volunteer holding the drink that would kill her, smiled stiffly with a steely, weary courage and said, 'Ready.'

Then, she took the paper cup, gulped back the poison and within minutes she was slumped forward, head lolling towards her lap, blood pooling in her beautiful lips, turning them from soft pink to a dark blue bruising black.

She had always said if she had to she would do it and when it came to it she did. We had to travel to another country because it was illegal in our own. It took months of preparation during which she would scream with rage about how complicated it all was and bite fleshy chunks out of me and herself.

The people who were helping her to die asked many questions about her history, her state of mind, her emotions. They couldn't help her to take her own life if she was anything less than sane and aware of the choice she was making. Dutifully I hid my scars in case they saw them and worked out that it was her that had caused them, which could lead them to question the sanity she was so skilfully presenting.

Capable of great charm, she convinced them she was simply a woman who valued life very much, who would never have made this decision had it not been for being diagnosed with a degenerative illness from which she was likely to suffer in a terrible way that she simply could not accept.

I went with her to the appointment with a psychiatrist who would vouch for her capability to make this choice. An elderly man with the smell of old cigars and a vocation. She talked with him in the calmest and most grounded of voices. He asked her questions about her life, and deftly she answered, painting the portrait of a woman who knew she had faults but nothing that meant she could not trust her own temperament. She said nothing about biting heads off or ripping holes into skin with her bare hands, just a story of a woman who had lived a long life, some joy, some grief, and who now simply wanted dignity.

At one point he asked her to write a sentence on a small piece of paper, 'Noun, verb, noun, please.' She wrote something and handed it to him. He looked at it, raised an eyebrow and said, 'Poetic, isn't she?'

I asked what it said. She growled but he didn't hear so he handed it to me. I looked at it, then to her. She'd written 'The sailor awaits the dawn.'

He was right, she was poetic.

After he had completed the interview with her, he asked if he could speak to me alone for a moment.

'She'll say terrible things about me,' she joked, lightly glancing at me, making sure I felt the weight of the glance. He guided me to another room.

Once we were on our own he sat, took his time before speaking, then asked me, 'What do you think?'

I thought of my mother alone in the other room, of all the years she had lived with being her, all the years of attempting care and tenderness and then tearing all that to shreds, hurting herself, hurting other people, taking love and shaking the bones of it, the way a dog shakes a stuffed toy, only to have to accept that was who she was, and that was what she had done, and having to start all over again. I thought of how tired she must be. How my father had left. But she never had. Even though the knowledge of all the damage she had done and all the shame she felt about it would always be waiting for her, lying at her feet from the moment she woke – the way you lay out a school uniform the night before, to be yet again picked up and strapped to her back, to be worn by her, carried by her, every step, every day.

I thought of how much she may now simply need to put it down and rest.

I thought of how she didn't want to be cared for. Didn't trust it. Didn't feel deserving of it.

'Do you approve of what she's doing?'

Behind him, his old clock ticked loudly, and in the distance an animal screeched a warning at another.

'I understand what she is doing,' I said, stopping myself from saying so much more.

'Good. That's right. That's all you need.' And with that he stood and walked back towards the room where Mum was waiting, preparing herself for death.

As we were leaving, we paused on his doorstep, she thanked him for his work and he blushed, reached out and took her hand in his. He wished her luck. He seemed taken by her. Moved by the person she was. Glad to have helped such a person.

But he didn't seem to see. Or if he did, he ignored it. If he had just looked a little closer at her hand in his, layer upon layer, decades of it, deep into the nail beds, so ingrained she could never wash it away. So much a part of her it had embedded itself and become part of her skin.

Dried blood under her nails.

The sailor awaits the dawn.

24

S HE HAS NO MUM. IT MUST BE HARD.
But having a mum can be hard too.

25

WE ARE WALKING HER HOME, THE THREE OF US. HER, THEM, me.

On our doorstep I notice the toe has gone, the leaf that was covering it now upturned. We walk on. Her, them, me. My child between us, connecting me to her and keeping us separate. For a while we don't say anything. It's dark. The sound of cars somewhere else. At the end of our road, I ask her, 'Which way now, love?'

She answers, half mumbles, 'Down here. But you really don't have to walk me, you know.'

'I want to,' I say, not really knowing what I want. I want to do the thing my child wants me to do, to make up for all the times I didn't. I want to get her away from us, to stop her taking them away from me. But I want them to be happy, and she now seems to be a part of that.

I walk next to them. They chat together about things at school. They laugh about a teacher, and both do an impression. I walk silently beside them, like a security guard. I want to join in. I want to be part of their huddle, to be invited in. Not to be this close and yet outside. But I am aware of my role.

We turn a corner.

'The next road is mine,' she says.

I see her tense, the laugh and lightness fading from her. And I can't help myself, I ask, 'Did your mum die?' I expect my child to be angry with me, for them to let me know with their eyes that I have overstepped a mark, that I'm out of order, and why couldn't I be one of those mums who would never ask that kind of question? But this doesn't happen. Instead, they look at her, as if they hope she will answer.

She is the one who looks angry, at them and at me. She looks past us and into the distance, like she is building up to saying something.

A siren wails past at speed. Someone calls out of a window.

Then a tabby cat stalks out in front of us, so big that for a moment I mistake it for a fox. It senses something in the darkness and turns to look. As soon as it sees us, it springs alert and starts hissing, back arching, fur standing on end, its mouth stretched wide, revealing pointlessly small fangs.

I feel shame. I try to calm my breathing.

Then, suddenly, she breaks away from us and lunges towards the terrified cat.

26

WHEN I WAS A CHILD, BEFORE DAD LEFT, ON A DAY WHEN Mum was in a light mood and seemed like she thought things were possible, Dad went to the pet shop and bought two baby rabbits.

He arrived home with the balls of pink-eyed grey fluff, a small wooden hutch and a bag of hay, which he set up in the garden while Mum stood close by, smiling and teaching me how to hold them.

All day I sat cross-legged on the grass, stretching the skirt of my dress over my knees so it made a sort of hammock, which the baby rabbits flopped about on while I fed them tiny chunks of carrot and small green grapes, which I skinned with my teeth to make it easy for them to swallow.

When it was time for me to go to bed, I placed them as gently as I possibly could in the hutch and then lay down on the grass on my stomach, so my mouth was level with the door. I whispered to them about how much I loved them and how I couldn't wait to see them the next day.

The moment I woke up I ran barefoot downstairs and out into the garden. As I got to the hutch, I felt something wet and slippery between my toes, I screamed and looked down. The grass around the hutch was a mess of grey fur, pools of blood and tiny blue red intestines.

My parents heard my screams and rushed into the garden. After they had managed to calm me down, Mum took me inside to wash the blood off my feet while Dad tidied up the rabbit corpses. Without speaking to me, he made another trip to the pet shop, returning with two more baby rabbits and a roll of wire fencing.

While he hammered and banged the wire around the hutch, I sat, as I had the day before, cross-legged, the babies in my lap feeding, but this time, a little more aware of their frailty.

When bedtime came it was hard to leave them. I made Dad check again and again that his fence was secure and told this new pair of rabbits repeatedly that they would be safe and I would see them in the morning.

I woke and headed straight for the garden. I stood in the doorway and through half-squinted eyes looked towards the hutch. Again, the grass around it was strewn with tiny baby body parts, torn fur, blood and intestines. The new fence ripped back in a snarling curl.

Mum was no longer in a light mood, and instead of comforting me, she shouted at me that I needed to stop making such a racket. Dad went again to buy more rabbits and fence. I think I actually asked him not to, suggested maybe we weren't a baby-rabbit kind of family. But he insisted we try one more time.

Two more babies were carried into the garden and

presented to me, their eyes pink and blinking. Oblivious
to what was coming. Oblivious to the fact that because my
parents had decided we should try to be the kind of family
that could keep pets, they were going to die.

Once again the wire was hammered into place. Dad not
speaking, driving the wooden poles into the ground with
blow after blow of a heavy block hammer. The thumping
echoing into the sky around, repetitive, like a death knell.

Once again I sat cross-legged feeding them. Their last
meal, peeled grapes and chunks of carrot that I chewed
and spat into my hand for them to nibble at. I felt I should
kill them there and then myself, put them out of their
misery, tear at their tiny throats with my teeth and put an
end to to all this pretending that we could be gentle, but
I could feel my mother watching me, could feel that she
was probably imagining tearing at my throat too, and so
once again I wished them goodnight, this time resigned
that I wouldn't see them in the morning.

Again I woke to death. .

Nobody decided it would stop or made any declaration
of the fact. Just this time both parents stood silently staring
at the ruptured fence and the blood-soaked hay. I didn't
even cry, so nobody had to shout at me and instead they
said nothing to me. They just calmly decided between them
who would tidy what and went about it routinely. I stood
watching as my mum scooped bloodied baby rabbit remains
into a dustpan and tipped it all into a black bin liner, and
my dad dismantled the hutch and chucked it onto a pile,
which he later set light to.

One day, as an adult, I asked Mum if she remembered
the rabbit story. She said I was cruel and went on to say

it had never happened. 'I would never have been naïve enough to try to keep pets.'

Then a few days later, she called me while watering her garden to say she *had* remembered the story and for the record she had always wondered if I had killed the babies. And then, changing the subject, she asked, 'If you're going to the garden centre, could you pick me up some soil?'

27

SHE IS CURLED INTO A BALL ON THE PAVEMENT, HER KNEES UP under her chin, head buried in them, rocking angrily.

A boy is missing.

I am standing back a little. They are kneeling next to her.

'It's OK. It's OK,' they are saying. 'We understand,' they keep saying.

They keep glancing to me. Wanting me to, what? What do you want of me? I nod back, a tight-lipped smile, trying to hold my ground. But I look at my child, caring, again. And I can't bear it. So, reluctantly I join them kneeling next to this young woman, sobbing and rocking and smelling of blood.

A couple walk past. Young, flirty, they look at us, exaggerate their movements to show they have to deviate from their desired route to get round us, letting us know how inconvenient we are.

I want to throw up all over the pavement in front of them. I want to ruin their evening. But I let them go as she has started to say something. It's muffled as her head is still buried in her knees, a murmur of something that sounds sad and small.

They look to me, urging me to help her. I want to do something they are thankful for, so I try.

'Hey, love, we can't hear you. You'll have to speak up a bit.'

They smile at me, and they do look grateful. I fill up with more wanting to please them, so I go on. 'Hey, love, we're here.' I pat her back, and my pat turns to rubbing, small reassuring circles, over and over. Across her hunched shoulders. Up and down her rigid braced spine. And I tell her, 'It's OK. It's OK. You're OK. We're here.'

28

WHEN I WAS A CHILD AND MUM WAS ANGRY, SHE WOULD leave letters addressed to me on my pillow. She was a letter-writer, maybe her way of protecting herself from ripping you to shreds. Written words keeping you one step removed from her teeth.

The letters used to tell me that she was no longer able to be my mother. Letters of resignation. They would tell me that being my mum was 'too difficult' and that she had to 'save herself' and so she was 'standing down'.

'I can no longer be your mother.'

I had no idea how you'd go about replacing a mother who had resigned. The fear used to burn through me like a house fire, nerves alight, panic in my chest, like a poison. I'd beg her not to stop being my mother, promise I would change, and she'd stand, watching me crying, screaming at her that I was sorry for whatever I had done to make her feel this way.

There are mothers who do, who actually leave.

But despite so clearly letting me know about her desire

to go, she never did. The next day I would sit at the table and she'd watch while I ate cornflakes and she stood drinking strong black coffee asking what time I had to be at school. I'd answer, and we wouldn't mention the letter, her attempt at resignation or my begging, we'd just carry on.

Until one day I left her.

I loved my mum. Despite it all, I loved her very much.

29

SHE'S IN THE BATH. OR I HOPE SHE IS. I RAN IT AND SHOWED her where all the soap-type stuff was, and I told her she should make herself at home and I left her in there.

They are sitting at the table staring at the bathroom door. I am standing by it holding two big clean towels listening to see if I can hear what she's doing, trying to seem like I'm not.

It took time but we persuaded her to come home with us. She was cold and shaking, mud covering the knees of her jeans.

They said, 'She can't go home like this.'

The girl nodded.

'Her dad will kill her, Mum. I mean it, seriously, he'll lose his shit.'

She nodded again.

'She has to come back to ours. You have to call him and say she's with us.'

She didn't nod now, just looked at me trying to work out whether I would say yes or no.

I said OK. I asked for his number and his name.

I dialled. I told them to stay where they were, sitting together on the pavement like toddlers, my child pushing leaves around in the gutter with their feet and telling her something that was making her smile, a grateful tear-stained smile.

I walked away from them and waited for him to answer. Hoping for a kind man.

'What? Who is this?'

In his tone I could smell something turned sour long ago.

'I'm with your daughter. She's not feeling very well . . .'

'Oh, yeah, is that what you call it?'

The sound of a TV in the background, too loud to watch, a sound to drown something out. A thought maybe.

'She can have a bath and I've fed her . . .'

'What do you want from me?' he said.

'There's a boy gone missing. All the kids are anxious, the school shut early . . . she came to our—'

'I know all this. What do you want? Are you accusing us? Are you the police? Are you the fucking police?'

His voice set fire like a lit match hitting nylon.

'Let me speak to him. Put him on the phone. Now!'

'To her you mean. I'm with your daughter,' I correct him, confused. I don't like this man. I want to hurt him.

'Him,' he growls. 'Let me speak to him.'

I breathe. Gulping at calm.

I look over to them together, still sitting on the pavement, leaning into each other, deep in the thick of chat.

And I see.

Tender. Gentle. My child. Her.

'You still there?' he shouts.

'Wait,' I reply, urge to protect.

But she looks over and sees me, and instantly she pushes herself up and walks towards me, ready.

'Your dad, he wants to talk to you. He sounds angry, love.'

But I see her grow taller the way you might to take something on – a punch, a truck, a tornado, your dad.

She takes the phone. Her voice so different from the shy half-whispers I've heard so far.

'Dad? With my friend . . . Yes, friend. No. I'm not. They're looking after me. Dad, you can't say that. Dad. Stop. Listen. You can't say that. Dad. I'm going to go. Dad, no. Dad. I'm going to stay the night.'

She glances at me, knowing I haven't agreed to this. I look back at her. And I feel myself nod.

'You don't know that, Dad. Them, Dad, they – fucking them! You're a wanker. Dad, you can't . . . Yes, the mum's OK with me! Dad, you can't just shout. Dad. Stop. Dad, I'm going. Do you want to talk with her again?'

And she holds out the phone to me. I can hear him shouting. I take it. She walks back to my child, their care for her visible, humming in the air like it has colour.

'You want him in your house, do you?'

'Yes, it's fine.'

'You know him, do you?'

'I know her, yes,' I lie.

'Fuck's sake. You know some boy's dead, don't you?'

'Missing I think . . . ' I hope.

A foot is missing a toe. There was a body bag in the park. I think it was me.

'He's a little piece of shit, you know.'

I say nothing. He says nothing. His television screams noise into the space between us.

'OK, I'm going to go,' I tell him. And I do. I hang up. One of my nails has punctured a hole in my palm. I wipe the blood on the inside of my cardigan and call to them both. 'OK, let's get home.'

And now she is in my bath, and they are waiting for her. And I am holding clean towels.

30

THERE'S A PHOTOGRAPH FROM WHEN I WAS SMALL, AGED around two, maybe three. I am running on a beach. Naked. There are no adults in the picture although one must have taken it. A little boy is running behind me. He has a look of resigned desperation, like he wants something he's never going to get.

My face is alive with a huge smile, not the kind of smile that comes from having beaten someone in a race or from sharing a joke. It's not a smile about being with anyone else, it's a smile for one and I look utterly lost in it. Running through the sea. My hair billowing behind me like flames. My feet kicking the waves, the white spray like sparks shooting out of my heels, my arms outstretched like I know they will soon be my wings.

For a while, Dad made photograph albums. They got more and more infrequent as I got older and stopped altogether when I reached about twelve. He secured the pictures with small triangles of tape at each corner and under them he'd sometimes write dates, and under a few he wrote captions.

Under this photograph he wrote 'Her First Boyfriend!'. I don't remember anything about this boy. In the photograph I don't even seem to be aware he's there.

But my dad saw something else.

31

WE HAD TO KICK THE DOOR IN. KICK IT RIGHT OFF ITS hinges.

They said, 'She's been in there too long, Mum.'

I said back to them, in a voice trying to sound grown up, 'Maybe she needs some time to calm down.'

'Mum! Too long!' Their voice rising with panic, like I should know what they meant. And I did know.

At first I knocked, and I said, 'Are you OK in there, love?'

She didn't answer. So I knocked again. 'Hey, can you hear me? Are you OK?'

Again, she didn't answer. So I banged with the side of my fist, and I said, 'Love, you're worrying us . . . Can you answer please?'

And then they shouted, 'We need to open the door, Mum. We need to fucking open it!'

I banged once more with my fist and then I just started beating the door with the flat of my hands, thumping, over and over and screaming to her. And then my child was next to me also beating and together we began to kick, and we kicked and we thumped, and we leaned back and threw our bodies into it, and then the door flew off its hinges.

32

THERE'S A MAN I WATCH SOMETIMES WHEN I GO SWIMMING. He comes with his daughter, to hold her baby. She's a young mother, she has a confidence and a lightness in her walk, even in the way she holds her child on her hip while she chats and drinks coffee from a paper cup, laughing with her dad. He's always nearby. Ready to help. When she wants to swim, he takes the baby from her. Bouncing it on his knees. Making it giggle by squeezing its feet or holding it high in the air and blowing up into its face. His daughter doesn't even look back, just turns away from them both, goes to the pool, drops herself into the water and swims lengths.

I watch him.

I watch for signs that he is not a kind man. I watch for moments that he might forget the baby or his daughter. That he might just get up and walk away. Or that while his daughter is swimming he might just let the baby crawl across the tiled floor towards the pool, where it would fall over the edge and sink to the bottom unseen.

I watch for the moments where he might be mistaking his daughter for another kind of woman in his life. Sometimes he touches her, combs the wet hair out of her eyes with his fingers, rubs her back when she looks cold. She once rested her head on his shoulder.

I watch them, trying to understand who they are.

33

WE HAD TO BREAK THE DOOR DOWN. ME AND MY CHILD, together. We used our combined force and smashed it right off its hinges.

A boy is missing.

I kill sometimes.

And this girl is in our bathroom.

34

THE WOMAN WHO LIVES IN THE FLAT DOWNSTAIRS FROM OURS is pregnant.

I don't really know her or her tight-faced husband. I make a point of not getting to know neighbours. If I think they might have heard me making strange noises then I apologize. I tell them things like 'It was a friend's birthday and I was drunk', or 'I ate something weird and I was sick', or 'I had a fight with my child's dad over money', or 'A friend asked me to dog-sit but the dog wasn't happy'.

I say, 'Sorry for the noise.' And I leave it at that.

I can tell they judge me for the excuses, but I can't care, although I do.

I've smiled at the pregnant one a few times and she doesn't seem to like it. She glances at me oddly, smiles a hard little smile back and hurries on.

Then one day she is in her garden. I can see her from our window. Her belly is fat and ready to pop. She has a blanket laid out on the grass; another woman has come over with a small baby. They have nappies and bottles and baby-type stuff laid out around them – some sort of practice run for when the neighbour's baby is born. The other woman's baby is crying, fast, furious siren-like sobs. Pregnant neighbour is trying to soothe the baby, awkwardly cuddling it and patting its back. She looks tense, her pats desperate. The other woman is smiling encouragement, but the baby doesn't stop crying.

Later, I hear some voices, a chat of goodbyes and then the front door goes. Then, a while later, I can hear the neighbour crying – full, angry, grown-woman sobs.

I take my shoes off and creep down to her door. I push my ear close. I don't do this so I can knock and go in and offer her comfort. Even if that was something I felt safe doing I am not sure what comfort I could give.

I do this so I can listen to another woman cry.

35

CAN BITE THROUGH BONE. YOURS OR MINE.

36

DON'T WANT THEM TO LOOK. DON'T WANT THEM TO SEE. THEY'VE seen terrible shit before, limbs ripped from sockets, veins pulled out of the skin as quick as you'd pull the cord through an anorak hood, bloodied lip, broken bone. They've seen too much, so if this girl is hurt, if this girl is injured, or worse, I don't want them to see.

I shout for them to turn around. Throw my arm towards them to push them out of the room. Enough blood, enough trauma, enough feelings too big for us both to carry but that we carry anyway because what else can you do? If this young woman has hurt herself, in our bathroom, that's not fair, that's not right, she chose us wrongly, we can't take any more, we've been through enough. She should have chosen one of those families who need shaking up to teach them some resilience, who've gone soft, like hands that never worked. We aren't those people.

'Don't look!' I scream towards them.

But 'Ssssh, Mum,' they reply, in their gentle whisper. 'Ssssh.'

I look to them and they're smiling. And they're looking. They have seen and they are smiling.

I look to the bath, no blood — just grey water with clumps of mud and gritty black eye makeup floating aimless on the surface like lost boats. But also, no her. Their friend is no longer in our bath. The mat is covered in wet footprints and my child has followed them and is now crouched down in the corner of the room, looking at me, still smiling.

I look to the floor in front of them, bare feet sticking out of the wrapped towel, tight around her like swaddling, curled in a ball, knees to chest, chin to chest, there she is, and miraculously she's asleep. A small snore, rhythmic like a purr.

'She hardly ever sleeps, Mum. She needs to sleep, this is so good. This is so, so good.'

37

A FEW YEARS AGO, I DECIDED THEY NEEDED TO TALK TO A therapist. I'd been to a few for myself. Yes, I felt judged by them, yes, I imagined them cleaning the room when I left and telling their loved ones how awful I was, what a lost cause, what a bad mum. But for the most part it helped. Stopped the worst. A rope thrown overboard just as I was about to go under. Sometimes I felt like I was screaming to them from beneath giant waves, my mouth filled with salt water and foam, while they sat warm and dry in armchairs calmly calling out the instruction 'Swim'.

But I hadn't drowned so it must have been of use, and so when I could see that my child was sinking I thought maybe they needed it too.

One time they'd fainted so I'd called an ambulance. We sat for hours in the waiting area of the hospital A and E. The chairs bolted to the floor, made of a hard curved orange plastic that never got warm and was impossible to sleep on. But my child still tried, pulling their knees up into the rigid back of one chair and resting their head in my lap while I sat upright next to them, waiting for their name to be called.

At one point their dad came. He paced in front of us, said he had to be up early for work, said to call him tomorrow to tell him what the doctors said, told our child to keep their chin up, didn't look at me.

When we'd both given up on being comfortable and had finally fallen asleep – my child curled in a ball on the floor under the seats and me still sitting upright, head lolling backwards so I kept jolting myself awake – their name was called.

They did tests, blood and that kind of thing, and they asked questions and then, after a few more hours, they said nothing appeared to be wrong, just that my child was underweight for someone of their age and needed to 'eat more cake'.

We went home, exhausted, on the bus in among early morning commuters, clean and ready, on their way to work. When we got in we fell onto our beds like a pair of drunks and slept through the entire day.

That evening I made dinner and watched as they didn't eat. I felt angry and scared that I might harm them. I hated to see them hurt themselves. But they were no longer at an age where I could tell them stories about food being trains and mouths being tunnels. I wanted to scream them into taking care of themselves, into not having a problem. Especially not having a problem that was, no doubt, the result of being my child.

But this time I was able to contain that urge and I didn't scream, and instead I pulled my chair up so close to theirs that our knees were touching and asked what was wrong.

But, really, I knew. And I knew they needed to talk to someone, and I knew that person wasn't me.

I found a lady. We went together on the train. Her house was small, with a high hedge around it in a suburban area right at the end of the train line. I tried to make the journey like an outing, pointing at interesting things from the window and buying us nice drinks from the café in the station.

When the woman answered the door, I was taken aback by her appearance. Despite being in her late fifties or even sixties she had very obviously dyed blonde hair piled high on her head in a ponytail and held in place with a ribbon, making her look like a confident little girl on her first day of school rather than a therapist.

My mum had always judged any older women who dyed their hair. Said they were in denial about ageing, which meant they were in denial about death, which meant they were in denial about life. I wondered how much a woman who couldn't accept her own greying hair and wore it in a ponytail could help us.

She was immediately warm and inviting to my child, while cold and business-like with me. I could feel them tense the moment we went inside her house, and they kept glancing at me when she spoke. She led us to the room she worked in. It was upstairs, and as we went we glimpsed the rest of the house. It was cluttered with belongings, floor space taken up with brightly coloured tufted rugs, large tangled plants with dusty leaves tumbling down shelves and staircases, walls packed with framed photos and paintings of flowers and butterflies and, in among them, wooden carved hearts, engraved cowbells on dust-covered faded coloured string and incense in holders, ashy and long since alight.

The room she took us to was small and there was too much furniture for its size. Under a window that looked out onto an overgrown garden, with a wind chime hanging from a dead branch clanking in the breeze, was a huge pink leather two-seater sofa, and in front of that, an orange-painted coffee-table with a box of tissues placed in the middle, one tissue standing on end like a fin ready for the first sign of a tear or a sneeze. On the other side of the table was a mauve velvet armchair that looked like a giant marshmallow.

She gestured that we should sit on the leather sofa, and once we had, she sank down opposite us into the armchair, her blonde hair standing out against the worn velvet. The walls were covered with more shelves, and the shelves packed with books with titles like *The Imperfect Mother*, *Peaceful Parent, Happy Kids* and simply *The Child*.

The first session she talked to us both, asked about their childhood. They were not keen to say anything bad about me, so I did, confessed that I was a less than 'peaceful' parent and, very definitely, an 'imperfect' one. I even told her about ripping off heads and tearing at limbs as I wanted my child to feel it was safe for them to say whatever they needed.

She nodded and punctuated my sentences by looking to them, saying things like 'That must have been very hard for you' and 'You must have felt very angry with your mother at that time'.

If they didn't reply, I would tell them it was really OK to do so, so then my child would say things like 'I guess it wasn't great'.

When she asked whether it was possible their father might attend a session, me and my child looked at each other. I said I'd try. She said it would be lovely if he could and returned to asking about their life with me and to nodding and commenting on how hard it must have been.

As we left, she hardly looked at me, and instead shook my child's hand and told them how nice it had been to meet them and how she looked forward to working with them.

It was arranged they would see her by themselves from now on. Each week I would travel with them on the train, pointing out the same things from the window and getting us the same nice drinks at the station. On the walk to her house, we would chat about random things, TV shows we liked, ones we thought were stupid, how your DNA is in your spit and how amazing it is that spit can carry facts about which country your granny came from. We'd spot dogs that we would like to own and notice cats watching us from windows.

We'd arrive at her door and the atmosphere would stiffen. She'd answer, say hello to them, nod in my direction and shut the door behind her. I'd walk the area for fifty minutes, looking in windows, staring at people's happy lives on my phone, waiting for them to finish, trying to manage my shame.

But one week their dad agreed he would come so we all went in together.

It had taken a few attempts to get through to him – he'd ignored quite a few of my messages – so in the end I'd sent an email with just the word 'Fire!' written in the subject.

He was reluctant; he wanted to help his child but questioned why I thought therapy was anything they needed, talked about kids needing to be kids, how he was concerned I was passing on ideas about them being broken and in need of fixing in some way. Said he was concerned that I was getting our child's needs mixed up with my own.

I had to say he might be right; had to say I could be wrong. I had to hold the blame and absorb his implication that in trying to help our child I was more than likely just making yet another mistake.

He arrived in a minicab. He was still wearing his work uniform. He got out and called to me. 'How long will we be?'

'We get fifty minutes,' I replied.

I thought about suggesting it might be good if he came with us for a cup of tea or something after, but I didn't.

I thought about ripping at his face with my teeth, but I didn't.

He leaned in the cab window, said something to the driver, handed him some money, looked at his watch and then he came over to us.

He ruffled our child's hair, told them he loved their shoes, made a joke intended for them about 'this all being pretty weird', nodded a cursory hello at me, clapped his hands and said, 'Right, let's do this thing, shall we?' Then he leaned across me and rang the doorbell.

Me and our child sat together on the leather sofa, he sat alone in the marshmallow armchair, and the therapist brought in a small wooden stool that looked like the kind you might sit on to milk a cow, which she perched on precariously. He was attentive and made jokes which she laughed at; he told her he really liked the colour of her walls. I stared out the window and listened to the wind chime clanging anxiously against the tree as she listed things she felt our child could do with having more of: attention, calm, protection from our problems, consistency. I listened as he vigorously agreed with her. I watched as he patted our child on the knee, saying, 'I love you, kid. You know that, don't you?' I noticed that he really seemed to be listening. That his agreement with her didn't seem at all fake. I ached for us to be unravelled and then pieced back together, to be fixed and able to start all over again.

At the end, standing on her doorstep, he shook her hand and thanked her.

Then, after she had shut the door and gone back inside and it was just the three of us, alone together, he hugged his child, looked at both of us and very earnestly, and I belive he meant it, said, 'I think that was good. I think that was a really good thing to do.'

He never came again.

After about six months of seeing the therapist, my child asked if they could stop. We were sitting at the station drinking our nice drinks, waiting for the train home, when they said it. 'Mum, I'd really like to stop seeing her.'

I looked at them and told them I thought it was important they had a place where they could talk about the difficulties of having me as a mother as openly as they deserved. I said they mustn't worry about that, that I wanted them to have it. That I was concerned they might really need this woman in their life, that I couldn't guarantee I could change enough for them not to.

'Yeah, Mum, I get that. Thanks. But she really seems

to not like you. And I feel like she really wants me to not like you too. I'm not sure how much it helps me to keep having to not like my mum. It's actually making me feel pretty freaked out and sad.'

And with that they leaned their shoulder into mine and asked if we could get some crisps.

They didn't go back to the woman.

38

AM SITTING ON THE FLOOR WITH MY BACK TO THE RADIATOR.
It's starting to burn, I don't mind. I am often cold. I want
to be warm. They are sitting opposite me with their back
to the wall. Between us she is still snoring. Her wet towel
rising and falling with each breath.

My child has been talking freely, like the world is a
good place and we are good people in it. Just the right
people in this bathroom right at this moment. So much to
say but all of it in a respectful whisper, not to disturb their
sleeping friend. They are telling me about how they first
met, how they noticed her because she reminded them of
us, of our family, our small two-person family, 'Something,
you know, something, Mum, she has that thing, the thing,
like you do, like I do.'

When they say this, I want to stop their flow. Their flow
is positive like it isn't a bad thing to be like us, but I heard
something I didn't want to hear.

'Like I do'. What did they mean?

I've never thought they were like me, always hoped and

told myself they weren't. Always believed that somehow they could be this close to me, but not the same as me. What do they mean, 'That thing, like you do, like I do'?

'But you're not like me.' And I do break their flow, I snap it in two like a dry twig.

They flinch.

'I am.' Their voice is so sincere it hurts to hear it, like a spoon being tapped on good glass. I want to run from it. I want to scream their words back into them, to roar them out of having been said.

She mumbles in her sleep. We both look. She sighs, then returns to a snore. My child looks back at me, their eyes full of such seriousness, locked on me. 'I am like you.' This is said with certainty and no self-pity or pain. Just a fact they want me to hear. They hold out their hands for me to look at their nails.

I feel like I am falling – through the earth to another sky, to an endless drop, to a nothing place, to a place where there is only falling and only ever will be. I can't answer. I can't speak.

I look at my child – at their face, not their hands. I won't look at their nails. I love this person, I love this person more than I will ever love any person, but I don't want them to speak any more.

'Mum . . .'

Between us she mumbles again, pulls her knees tighter into her chest but doesn't wake.

The radiator behind me is scorching my skin, I push against it even harder. My child is smiling at me, willing me to smile back.

39

I T WAS GREECE, SUMMER, JUST US, AS EVER.

I'd booked quickly on a credit card, an attempt to buy us some good after a bad time. We swam in the sea and watched sand-coloured fish fussing between our toes and did the thing where we would stand in the water facing each other and they would step into my cupped hands and bend their knees while holding onto my shoulders and I'd count to three and bounce, watching their smile grow with anticipation, and then on three I'd fling my hands upwards and throw them as hard as I could into the air, and they would fly, arching their spine in a rainbow, sending tiny fish scattering in all directions as they flew into the water in a backwards dive.

Maybe I didn't fling them as high as a dad might have, but they didn't know that. We did it over and over again.

We saw stray kittens sleeping in a tree trunk, feeding from their worn-out mum, and drove around in a golf buggy faster than the sign said we should. A normal family with a mum, dad and a son, and no scars on their arms, made friends with us on purpose in the hope our children would play together. They started saving us a space on the beach next to them.

Some days we had to hide from them because they kept asking questions about our life and we both got worn out pretending to be the kind of people they understood. On those days we took the bus to other beaches and spent money I didn't have on adventures.

We were given lifejackets and a talk on safety. We were strapped into a harness and driven, just us two, out to sea by a bored-looking young man in a dirty white speedboat.

Once the shore had become horizon the bored guy stopped the engine and all sound fell away and we bobbed about on the waves, inhaling diesel and silently nervous of what was coming next.

The joyless young man gestured for us to get into the water.

We could have done with some joy. I felt a rush of rage towards him. But my child looked scared so I faked excitement and confidence and hand in hand we jumped into the vast empty sea. The harness meant they had to sit in my lap; we waited, drifting about in the water, like a pair of stacking chairs. I clamped my arms tightly around their waist. They leaned back into me, trusting. Who else did they have to trust?

The man shouted a monotone countdown – six, five, four. The engine of the boat screamed, and once more the air was filled with a booming rush, a burst of diesel smell, and the boat sped away from us. A jolt of rope. Harness pulled tight. The parachute behind us that had been lolling in the sea like drifting underpants suddenly flew up into the sky behind us. For a moment we were dragged. The water battering us, tugged along on our bums. Breath punched backwards into our lungs. I could feel their body tense with fear. I held them tight, called into their ear that this was 'brilliant', but my words were snatched away and hurled out to sea.

Then, suddenly, the battering stopped, and the water shot away from us and we were being fast flung up into the sky towards the boiling sun, the stupid, bored, joyless man in the boat becoming smaller and smaller.

Us – together – flying.

Away from smiling for strangers and having to hide who we were. Birds at eye level, wings outstretched, winking at us, saying yes.

My child turned and looked at me, their eyes alight with awe and fear.

I stuck my thumb up at them. 'Good?'

They grinned, breathless, back at me. My brave child – so much fear felt already in their only ten years. Thumb up. 'Good!'

Us above the world, soaring.

40

PUSH THEIR OUTSTRETCHED HANDS AWAY, FOLDING THEIR fingers into their palms so I can't see their nails. 'You are not like me! You mustn't say that. You're nothing like me.' My voice is raised. I don't care. Let her wake. This sleeping person I am suddenly meant to give refuge to. No. I don't want to. Fuck off. Leave us alone. Leave my child alone. Leave me alone. My child has never wanted to be like me before, but now you come along, and they're saying this. I want you out.

'Mum, sssh, please.'

But I am standing. 'You are not like me!'

She jumps awake, surprised to find us in the room with her. She pulls the damp towels tight around her and my child tells her, in a voice that shows their allegiance is with her, 'Get behind me!' while moving so they are standing in front of her and up to me. 'Stop it, Mum. Stop!'

I can do all this, carry this shame, live with the rejection and the losing loves and the losing friends and the biting chunks out of myself and the constant repairing and letting doctors think they've solved me when all they have done is sedate me. I can do all of that because I do not think my child is like me. Because I tell myself that it has not been passed on. That it ends in me.

'What happened? I'm so sorry. Is this my fault?' she asks, quiet from behind their knees.

'This has nothing to do with you. You are fine!' they tell both her and me.

My breath is slow. Not a calming slow but a burning slow. In, out, in, out. Vision blurring.

'Stop, Mum, please stop.'

I want to pass out, I want to fall to the ground like a cut-down tree where I will stay forever until moss covers me and animals make nests in me, and I lie there being no harm to anyone.

I can't speak for the fire I will spit. Cannot move for the violence I may inflict. I stand. I breathe. This is the best I can do.

I know you want better from a mother, perfection, cupcakes, knitting, boundaries, unconditional everything, positive mirroring, patience, maturity, self-control, humility, consistency, handmade toys and not too much sugar. Resilience, persistence, clarity, homemade jam, perfect flipped pancakes, a good talk on drugs that neither terrifies nor encourages, well-planned holidays, always plasters and disinfectant in the cupboard, a mother who gives all she can, while not forgetting her own needs, and who will never tell you her problems and will never burn out, a good recipe for pasta sauce, the right gifts on birthdays, not too much not too little, more more forever for always. More.

But this is all I have.

The not tearing us to pieces is all I have to give right now.

41

M Y LABOUR WAS TWENTY-TWO HOURS. MY WATERS DIDN'T break like they do in films. I'd wanted them to, maybe in a supermarket aisle or on the escalator to the Underground, a river trickling from me down the silver staircase and running between the legs of all the commuters. I imagined that maybe I'd look down at the puddle below me and gasp and gently say, 'I think it's happening,' and then he'd hold my hand and I'd waddle to the car like a majestic goose while he reminded me to breathe.

Instead I was scared I hadn't felt my baby move for a few hours and I had a bit of a strange pain in my pelvis. I was alone. He'd gone back to stay at his mum's as we'd had a row about whether he'd looked at the young guy in the takeaway in an aggressive way. He had. He said he hadn't.

I didn't have my own car, so I got a cab to the hospital. They hadn't let me into the labour ward as they said I wasn't officially in labour. I wanted badly to be in there with the monitors and the other swollen women. But I'd been sent to A and E, where I sat on a cold plastic chair with a man who'd cut his thumb off opening a tin. The thumb lying on the seat next to him in a little sandwich bag resting on some bloodied ice-cubes, like Sleeping Beauty in the glass case. A woman who had given herself a black eye with a dog-lead fastener was telling the story over and over into her phone, 'I just took it off the hook and it swung and smacked me in the eye. Could have taken it out! It's totally black, black and yellow – stupid fucking dog.'

The nurse on the desk was kind enough but the doctor who examined me clearly thought I was wasting hospital time. She did an internal examination and said I wasn't even three centimetres dilated and should have stayed at home watching something nice on telly. She then made a rough swiping movement with her fingers around the inside of my vagina and about twenty minutes later my contractions were coming every five minutes and I thought I was going to pass out with the pain.

I found out later she'd given me a 'sweep', a procedure intended to bring on labour when it isn't coming naturally. They're not meant to do this to you without permission or warning. But she was obviously fed up with me for turning up at the hospital just looking for reassurance and company and decided to teach me a lesson. And by the time I found out this was what she had done my baby had been born and I was a mother and had no strength to complain.

I never caught up with the speed of my labour. Their dad arrived a few hours into it. He had a look on his face like he was being forced to watch a horror film he had absolutely no interest in seeing. He avoided my eyes, and when he could stared out of the window or up at the ceiling.

I shat myself. I tried to get onto all fours like women do in natural-birth films, but by then I'd had so many top-ups on the pain relief I couldn't feel my legs and they slid apart like a just-born goat trying to stand and my arms gave way under me so I landed on my chin and gave myself a nosebleed. The nurse and their dad had to lift me and flip me over, like a heavy pancake.

I landed with a thump and shat myself again. Their dad left the room. He said he felt sick and glanced at me like I had done something terrible to him.

My baby didn't want to come out, they kept telling me. Didn't want to 'drop'. They monitored the heartbeat on a machine attached to a speaker so it echoed round the grim grey bloodstained room like a watery drum. I loved that sound. They told me the baby sounded calm, I was pleased, but they said it was too calm. 'This baby is not engaging in being born,' they told me, as if this was my fault. 'Your baby is trying to not come out. It's too comfy in there. You need to tell it it's time to leave.'

But I didn't want to. If they were comfortable, I didn't want to drag them into the world and all that is so uncomfortable about being in it.

In the end they dragged my baby out with a sort of Hoover that sucked its head into a red-raw point shape that took days to go down.

I tore, ripped. The doctor stitched me up the way you might an old canvas bag you no longer care much about but can't bring yourself to chuck out. I couldn't feel any pain – I was still so numb – but I could feel that with each tug of a stitch the doctor pulled me a little further down the bed, like a heavy fish on a line being dragged onto the beach.

They stitched me and pulled the placenta from me, the nurse's whole hand rummaging around inside me, like she had lost some keys at the bottom of a shopping bag. They laid my bloodied mucus-covered baby on my chest. We lay together while they mopped up and packed away machines. It felt like we were lying in the middle of a traffic accident.

Later that night we were alone, in a small side room we'd been put in due to something bad, which I now can't remember, just me and my tiny pointy-headed baby.

Their dad had left a couple of hours after they were born saying he'd come back tomorrow.

The day faded and evening arrived. The first evening of us.

The ward outside was dark. I couldn't sleep. When I peed I felt like my whole body was made of shards of broken glass. I cried with the pain, and the water in the toilet was filled with red. A nurse had come in to give me an injection: I had a blood group that meant my baby could reject me or something. Their blood was stronger than mine, or something. I showed her the toilet bowl; she tutted and flushed it. She told me the blood in my pee was normal and I should only call for her if I started to 'pass meat'.

Then she left us alone and nobody else came in.

I sat on a rubber ring, so my stitches didn't touch the bed. I held my baby that didn't feel like my baby. I couldn't feed it as my dry nipple just fell out of its mouth.

I stared at my baby's face and ached to know what to do.

I was hungry. I wanted to ask if someone could help us.

I laid my baby on the bed beside me and lowered myself onto my feet, wincing with every movement, glass-shard stabs, bruised muscles, split skin. I had no slippers and no nightie. I was wearing two faded hospital gowns, one with the gaping hole at the back as it should be worn and the other over it with the back at the front to cover the open back of the first gown. The ties dangled around me like unravelling bandages.

I lifted my baby and padded on the cold sticky hospital floor to the door. In the distance I could hear whispering, a woman crying, even further away traffic, a world. The corridor was lit in a dull green neon. Carrying my baby, shuffling with pain, I walked. Doors were closed. I was nervous to knock. Sometimes behind them, voices or snoring. The nurses' station was empty, an abandoned cup of tea the only sign anyone had been there. I found a small kitchen, an empty fridge, a cupboard, a small collection of single-serving cereal boxes, the kind you get in hotel buffets.

I gripped my baby under my armpit, with my elbow resting on my hip to secure them in place, and clumsily ripped open a box of unnaturally orange cornflakes. I shovelled them into my mouth, dropping a couple on my baby's head. They blinked and the cornflakes looked like giant falling leaves.

I felt dizzy and sick. I wanted to get back to our room.

I tidied the packet into the bin and made my way back into the corridor. As I did, I noticed a thin red line wiggling its way drunkenly along the floor towards us. I followed its trail like Hansel and Gretel. It came from the direction we had come from, then went behind us into the small kitchen with the bare cupboards where it spun around in a few dizzy circles then followed us out, coming to a stop at my feet. I looked down at a small dark oval puddle.

Later when we were back in our room, precariously perched on the rubber ring, aching for sleep but terrified to close my eyes in case I missed something my baby needed, the tutting nurse pushed open the door with a bang and threw a large white padded sanitary towel onto the end of my bed. 'You made a mess. Someone had to clean it.'

The door clunked shut behind her as she left.

My baby whimpered. I tried to feed them again, pulling at their tiny chin with the flat of my thumb to open their mouth and pushing my giant nipple between their bony pink gums. My breast felt like it had turned to rock, veins stood up on it like dark blue rivers seen from the sky. My skin was hot, and hurt when I touched it.

My baby sucked. My body felt a hundred different sparks of electric pain. My mind raced and went numb, then raced again. We stayed like this, locked together, alone, all night.

42

I AM IN MY ROOM.

I've locked the door. I am pacing. Prowling. Heart racing. Wanting to smash, to howl, to rip, to tear. Outside I can hear them whispering, my child and her. They are whispering about me. Words float in – 'help', 'medication', 'scary', 'Mum'.

I crawl into my bed, under the duvet, under the sheet onto the bare mattress below it. I would crawl inside the mattress if I could. Curl up like one of its springs and stay there.

I don't want to hurt my child. I don't want to hurt this girl, because to hurt this girl would hurt my child. I bite into my pillow. My mouth fills with feathers. I swallow them hoping they will fill me up and make me soft but instead I choke and vomit – a pile of wet feathers sticky with bile and no good for flying.

I push my face into the mattress and scream into it.

They knock at my door.

'Leave me alone,' I say.

They knock again. 'Let us in, Mum. Please.'

And her, 'I'm sorry if I've caused any trouble.'

'No, stay away from me,' I beg. 'Please, just leave me alone. You haven't done anything wrong, but please leave me alone.'

'Mum, we want to help. We don't want you to be on your own. Please.'

And I do want to be helped. And I don't want to be on my own. But if I let you in, I can't promise, have never been able to.

My window is open. I go to it. Climb onto the sill. Leap. Maybe I will fly. I crash to the ground. Air punched out of my lungs. I am sick again. More feathers. I push myself up. Hands grazed. Bare feet.

And I begin to run.

43

DURING MY PREGNANCY, ONE EVENING WHEN ME AND THEIR dad were attempting to be normal, we dressed up and went for dinner. It was a restaurant that only served mussels and beer. I thought I'd read somewhere that pregnant women shouldn't eat shellfish, but there was a feeling, like in that moment we simply liked each other. We were smiling and managing to be in each other's company with no blood or severed bone so I decided that I'd eat the mussels and hoped it would be OK.

We had to rush to the hospital. When we arrived, the place was packed. The nurses put a monitor to my stomach and my baby's heartbeat thundered out around the room, electric and watery. They said our baby seemed OK but that I should be taken to a ward so they could keep an eye on us, but, they explained, since they were so busy, they were having trouble finding someone to take me there. Their dad had worked as a hospital porter for a while to support himself through uni. He told the nurses he could do it.

Said firmly, 'Just get us a trolley, please!'

They did. I climbed onto it and propped myself up cross-legged, my belly on my lap, my arms wrapped round it. They told him the way and he began to push. Him pushing me, me carrying our baby, like I was a fragile pot being transported to a better position. The hospital was made up of a collection of buildings, spread out all down one street, and underground there was a tunnel, connecting them all, strip-lit, cold brick walls, painted long ago, now peeling and cracked, separated by big doors that you could crash your back against to make them swing open.

As we approached one of the doors, he ran from the head of the trolley behind me to the foot of the bed in front of me, and pulling with one arm, he flung his back and the raised elbow of his other arm against the doors so they flew open.

A man once said to me, 'I know you. You see a light at the end of the tunnel, and you just build more tunnel', a metaphor intended to point out to me that this man saw how difficult I found it to stay with the good things in my life, and because of that, he felt, I was now manufacturing more darkness.

But being in this tunnel with my baby and their father was a kind of good thing I was happy to stay in forever, their dad being so kind, so capable. Me feeling like I was almost worth looking after, and our baby, with their strong heart beating, defying the dangers of our stupid choices. Us, a mum and a dad, not mature, just kids really, kids with a kid of our own that we were now racing under-ground together to keep safe.

I imagined we'd make a great family. I thought we'd be

like the couple in that song, that we'd throw homework on fires and buy shoes and trumpets. Yes! I thought. Stay, be with us, I thought. You won't be sorry! We can do this. And it will be good. It will be so good.

44

RUN. I AM RUNNING. I DO NOT STOP RUNNING.

A boy is missing.

I am capable of terrible things.

You are not like me.

I love you. I love you. I love you. But.

45

THERE HAD BEEN A MAN.

Another.

I knew straight away I should stay away from him as he told me in detail how much he hated his mum, how much she had failed him, how weak she was, how selfish she was, how much she had damaged him.

I asked him about his father, reaching for some balance, but he dismissed the question. 'My dad is fine, he's kind of just a dad, he's had to put up with Mum a lot, which is hard for him but he's OK. It's her . . .'

Women like me should not get involved with men who hate their mothers.

But I don't think I ever went out with a man who said his mum was a good mum. They all seemed to have had terrible mums and they told me about them quickly, as if I was in some way responsible, and I didn't question them. In fact, I very often said things like 'Sounds so hard' and 'I'm so sorry', while thinking to myself – my poor child has a terrible mum too.

I also wanted to scream into their faces, to kick them over cliffs, to explode their stories, to stand up for their mums. But instead I punished myself for thinking such things and nodded along while they vilified the women.

Terrible mothers and terrible past girlfriends, lists of so many women who had failed them and how. Within weeks I would start to rip at my own skin and spit foamy bile and tear heads off living things in front of them and then they would say, 'You are just like my mother, you are just like my ex, you are mad.' Which I had expected and accepted.

It's not normal to bite a head off.

This new man was screaming, 'You're fucking mad.' I was crying, begging him not to leave, punching myself in the face and saying he was right about me. Then somehow in amongst all this we had sex. That often happened. They told me I was mad, then we had sex.

This time he came inside me; I'd asked him not to.

The next day I had to take a pill.

The pill made me sick. Blood came and it wouldn't stop and all I could think of was biting and harming.

I bled for nine weeks and every night, once my child was asleep, I bit blood-soaked chunks out of myself and had to restrain myself from more killing, which at times I failed at.

During this time, the man decided we should go on a trip. I didn't want to lose another person I had convinced myself might make our small family bigger, so I decided I needed to become a fun woman on a weekend away, not a bleeding, biting one. I sent my child to their dad's, promising them that when I got home, we'd go together on other trips with this man.

The day we left the man handed me an envelope of cash and said, 'You can buy yourself something while we're there.'

He booked us into a hotel with views of the city and a DJ in the bar, even at breakfast. I bled onto the expensive white sheets and had to apologize to a woman who came to clean the room who looked ashamed on my behalf and waved her hands in my face to make me stop talking.

He wanted to go to a sex shop. I'd never been into one: sex had always made me cry, had never felt like a safe place; it was something I did in the hope I'd be wanted afterwards, not a thing I did for pleasure. I was ashamed of this, I knew for other women it was different and fun, I admired them for it, so I pretended I had a light heart about it and hoped one day that lightness would arrive.

Inside the shop, as he picked up various penis-shaped toys and chatted with the lady behind the counter about prices and the weather, I felt afraid and as if I was fading.

He bought a vibrator and a pair of nipple tassels. I didn't want to jump up and down for anything, let alone to make my aching breasts spin, but he smiled and handed them to me wrapped in brown paper with a pink ribbon. Back at the hotel he suggested I try them on. I wanted to ask if we could wait until I'd stopped bleeding, but when I went to speak all the words I'd ever known had disappeared and I just howled and curled up in a ball in the corner of the jet-black tiled shower room.

He took us to a strip club. In the lift on the way down to the hotel foyer I felt as if my whole body had filled with smoke, and I no longer existed.

In the club I smiled and clapped along as the women

danced and removed their clothes and he pushed money into their underwear. They were beautiful women of all different sizes and shapes. Some in feathers, one with an umbrella.

The next morning, before we left for the flight home, I spent the money he'd given me on a huge bag of sweets for my child and a long black coat for myself that looked like it belonged to an undertaker.

On the plane I bit large foamy chunks out of the seat in front of me, screamed into the air-conditioning vents and chewed holes into my fists. He called a steward over and asked him to help him restrain me.

Together they did. I let them. It was a relief.

I had to drive us home. Despite his age he'd never learned to. I had learned to drive at sixteen, desperate for escape routes. I kept wanting to accelerate as fast as I could, to drive off the road and straight into the trees lining the side of the road, but I knew my child was at home waiting so I pulled over onto the hard shoulder and crawled on my hands and knees into a tangled bush where I hoped I might crumble and turn to mud.

He shouted at me to come out and eventually, with dirt covering my knees and blood in my mouth and underpants, I did, and I drove us home, breathing as hard as I could while begging myself not to even look at the beckoning trees.

At home I held onto him and thanked him for staying.

He left.

He didn't return calls. Sent a message saying it was over and that he'd been advised by a therapist that I was not good for him.

I tore at myself. Spat at myself for losing us another possibility. My child was scared and told me not to hurt myself. Told me that we were fine on our own, that they didn't care about trips with that man.

I called their dad and told him to come and get them again. He came, didn't look at me, muttered something about not being able to 'do too long', took our child and their two little bags of belongings, clothes in one, toys in the other, and when the car had turned the corner at the end of our street I went back in the house and took pills.

46

T'S RAINING. I AM SOAKED. A THICK HEAVY RAIN LIKE IT WILL never stop. I keep running.

In my pocket my phone rings. I let it. I know who it is by the ringtone. It's the one I chose for them, for my child. It's the one called 'Alien'. My alien child. My child from me but not of me. My child, made by my blood and my bones, held and fed in my stomach by my muscle and my organs but not like me. Different from me. Alien to me. Kinder than me. Wiser than me. Not going to rip like me. Not going to tear like me. Not to destroy like me. No, not like me. No, please, not like me. I want to answer. I want to let them tell me to come home. To tell me I am OK. I want to run back to them and this new friend of theirs who needs us, to curl up with them and feel warmth with them.

I want it so much.

But I mustn't.

A boy is missing.

We have scars.

I am the cause.

I am capable of terrible things.

I run. I keep running.

47

I WOKE UP BEING SICK. THE PUKE BITTER AND BURNING WITH chemicals. My body fighting them.

I lay on the floor. The ceiling spun above me. My stomach started to spasm, muscles contracting. I curled into a ball. Wretched, puked more. Bright yellow.

I had a friend then. She isn't any more. She phoned to ask for a recipe I'd once told her about. She heard my voice, asked what was wrong.

I lied, said maybe I had food poisoning, told her not to worry.

She said I sounded bad. I said I would be fine. She said I didn't sound like I would be. I told her what I had done. She called an ambulance.

The paramedics were a young man and woman. They asked if anyone was with me. I said no. They asked what I had taken.

I started to cry. I was ashamed. A grit-filled shame, which felt like wet cement, and I knew would set. I felt stupid, selfish, like I was taking up space in the world that another type of human could make better use of.

The man drove and the young woman sat next to me and held my hand, which she patted every now and then. When we arrived at the hospital and they were leaving me with the nurses, the young paramedic woman said goodbye and told me she hoped I would be OK.

I didn't want her to go. I wanted her to stay holding my hand and patting it for the rest of the night, maybe for some days, weeks, years. If I wasn't going to die then I wanted to wake up every day with this young woman at my side, not as a partner, nothing as difficult as that, she would just be sitting in the chair by my bed reading a book or doing a crossword. Maybe she would notice I'd woken up and acknowledge me with a nod and a smile. She didn't even have to be my friend, we didn't have to speak, just while she had been holding my hand, I had felt a gentleness, and it felt like the kind of thing that over time might be able to soften cement.

I watched as she walked away through the double doors back out into the ambulance bay and the night beyond it.

The friend came to A and E. She was wearing a fake fur coat and a dress with red velour hearts on it, on her way to somewhere or from. I had a cardboard bowl on my lap.

I kept throwing up into it although there was nothing left to come out, my body determined to keep me alive even though I had tried to kill it.

The friend asked how I could do such a thing. How could I think this was an answer to anything?

I said nothing, just spat into the bowl trying to get rid of the poisonous taste filling my mouth. She paced, even though there was an empty cracked brown-leather chair next to me.

After a while she checked her phone and said she had to go. She patted my foot as she left.

I never saw her again. I understood.

A few hours later I was taken to a ward. A man was crying out from his bed, 'Nurse, Nurse, help me, Nurse.' The nurse would go to him, there would be whispering, the nurse would walk away, he'd begin to cry again. 'Nurse, Nurse, help me, Nurse.'

I was attached to a drip. The drip attached to a metal pole on a set of small metal wheels so I could push it with me if I walked. I was put in a corner of the ward. The curtains drawn around me. They were made of an old thick cotton fabric covered with a faded pattern of huge, intertwined orange flowers. The stems twisting and knotted together, the flowers fully open, like mouths singing, screaming or saying 'aaah' ready to be examined for ill health.

A young male nurse came to my bedside and introduced himself. Told me his name. I've forgotten it. I'm ashamed of that. He was kind. 'This is your drip,' he said. 'It's attached to you so don't pull on it.' His voice was matter of fact but gentle. 'You need anything, you call.'

'What is the drip doing?' I asked.

'Pumping the crap out of you so your poor liver can recover.'

'Will it work?' I asked. 'Sorry, I'm wasting your time.'

'Not at all,' he said, neither committed to his answer nor dismissive of my statement.

'Could I still die?' I asked.

He carried on cleaning items on the trolley of medication he had with him. He answered me without stopping his work. 'We don't know yet. It'll take a few days for us to know.' He looked up at me. 'Sleep. Let this do its work.'

He tapped the pole of my drip, which tinkled like a bell.

'You want these closed?' he asked, referring to the orange flower curtains.

'Yes, please.'

So he did and he left.

I lay wide awake, staring at the flowers. Sometimes they were screaming mouths, sometimes planets on fire, sometimes severed heads, babies floating into space.

I counted them, lost track and counted again.

The man called out for the nurse. Hours passed, a day passed. The young man would come in, take my blood and go.

I walked with the drip, pushed it in front of me. I passed the crying man. He was curled in a ball on his bed, his bare back sticking out between the fastenings of his gown, pale sagging skin covered in browning age spots, spine curved and ridged, his arms wrapped round his head in the brace position like the drawings in an aeroplane safety pamphlet. 'Nurse, help me,' he called over and over.

I walked the corridors. I found a window. Counted buildings.

I tried to work out where my child was, tried to map in my mind the journey I'd have to take to get to them. I'd only been inside their dad's flat a few times. I'd not been invited in so I had stood awkward and unwanted in the hall. Glimpsed a flat-screen telly. Toys they already had at mine. Many new, still un-played with, still in their boxes.

I tried not to imagine what my child was thinking, where they thought I was. Called to them in my head and hoped they heard but wondered if they'd want to.

I went back to my bed, pulled the orange flower curtains closed around me, cutting off the ward outside. I lay in amongst the mutating flowers and imagined my child forgetting me. How another woman might take my place and they'd love her with far more ease, and she'd be only good.

The kind nurse stuck his head in. He was wearing a red puffer coat over his uniform. It looked good against the flowers. 'I'm going home. You'll be here when I get back, yes?'

I nodded. Not really knowing, my liver was still deciding.

'Good, good,' he said, and went.

I walked again with my drip; the man continued to cry out; I stood at the window and imagined I could fly. I came back and counted the flowers on the curtains – 292 if you included the half-flowers along the edges, 286 if you didn't.

In the evening the nurse came back. He pulled back the curtains with a rattle and wheeled in his trolley. 'Hey, still here I see. Good, good. Exciting day?'

'Yes,' I said, playing along, wanting to ask more about how my liver was doing but not wanting to bother him or maybe scared to know the answer. 'And you?' I asked instead.

'Very. I slept, did some laundry, watched a cartoon with my son, ate pasta, came here.'

'How old is your son?' I asked, not wanting to talk about children because I missed my own and felt weighed down with guilt but knowing I would seem even more selfish if I didn't.

'He's four. You got kids?' he asked while preparing a syringe.

I nodded. 'Yes. One.'

He took my pulse, took my temperature and then some blood. 'Right, well, let's hope these bloods are looking better – we need to get you home.'

I looked away. Drowning in shame. Didn't want him to shout at me, to tell me what a stupid, useless woman I was. But he didn't shout.

'What's your kid's name?' he asked, laying the bottles of my blood side by side in a cardboard tray, as if they were sleeping or dead things.

I told him.

'Nice,' he said, and left.

I called my child's father. He asked where I was. I could hear a cartoon blaring in the background. I said I hadn't been well. That I was in hospital for a bit. He said his mother was sick as well and he needed me to take our child back as soon as possible. He said his mother might die and waited for me to show suitable compassion. I tried.

I didn't dare tell him they were still checking my blood, that it was still possible my liver would fail, that it was still possible that I'd die too, and that it would be my own fault, and I'd never be able to take our child home, and then both him and our child would be without their mothers. I didn't dare point out to him that if we both died he'd have nobody to ask for help.

Instead, I said I'd let him know as soon as I was well. Then I said, 'Please tell them that I . . .' But he hung up before I finished the sentence.

I walked again, up and down, pushing my drip. Its wheels

smooth and fast on the laminate floors. The nurse saw me. He was sitting at his station writing up notes or something. I wheeled my way over to him.

'Have you had my blood back yet?' I asked.

He didn't look up from his paperwork. 'Not yet, no.'

I didn't move. Didn't want to. Needed him.

'Why are you asking?' he said quietly, looking up at me for a moment.

'I want to go home and look after my child.' And I wanted it more than anything I have ever wanted.

'Good, good,' he said, looking back down to his work.

When, three days later, they told me my liver was OK and I would live, I made a decision, a pact with myself – a rule or something like that – I'm not good at sticking to things but this was something I was determined I would.

'Don't do that again. Not ever. It's never the right thing to do. And never leave. They are allowed to go. When the time is right. Like children are meant to. They can leave you. But you can't leave them. You stay.'

48

RUNNING.

I may have broken a bone when I jumped. Or twisted something. One of my ankles keeps giving way. Running and limping. I run past a mother pushing her child in a stained pink pushchair. The mother looks frightened of me, she instinctively hurries across the road to get away, but her child laughs, and as they pass, the child reaches out a hand towards me as if I am a tame animal that she can pat or stroke. I show my teeth.

The child retreats into the back of her pink chair, turning her face into its hood.

I keep running.

It feels like a bone in my ankle may push down and break through the skin and come out the sole of my foot. But I keep running. The pain makes sense. Is right.

And I think of my mum.

I want to run to my dead mum.

I want to climb into her arms, and I want her to rock me and say things like 'There, there, my love' and 'It's OK' and 'You're OK' and 'I'm sorry' and 'It's over now, all over now'.

And then, although I am an adult and heavy and wet, soaked through, I want my mum to carry me. I want her to take me to a room. And in the room there will be another woman. My mum's mum, born in Cork, orphaned at nine, travelled to the East End of London in search of work, had her baby at sixteen. Worked during the day in a boiled-sweet factory and at night as a pub singer, singing songs about leaving jungles she had never been to and would never go to.

My mum's mum, whose husband jumped ship during the Second World War to remarry in Australia, faking a letter home telling her he had died and leaving her alone to raise their daughter.

And there will be another.

My great-grandmother, born in Odesa, fled to London with her babies during the First World War after her husband was killed. Worked cleaning for and raising the children of a wealthy family in Kensington. Who was so afraid of her own children being unable to afford food that when she died, in a tiny flat in a place called Jubilee Mansions many years later, they found her bed was floating a foot off the floor, precarious, balanced on the piles of tins and packets of food she had collected and hoarded under-neath it.

And they will stand with my mum, my mum born in East Ham. My mum who, when she was evacuated during the Second World War, was so dirty and her hair so full of nits no kindly country family took her in, even though she was only five, so she slept alone in dark church pews wrapped in old blankets, imagining ghosts. My mum, made a 'ward of court' and taken in by teachers and strangers aged nine, as her father had gone and her mother was only a child herself and simply couldn't cope. My mum, who throughout her adult life repeatedly said that she had no childhood memory of being 'held'. My mum, who was called mad by the father of her children even at her own funeral but who raised those children the best she could through all her wild and heartbroken, while he left to remarry and to become father to more children, sending her money that he called her greedy for taking.

My mum, who nursed her mum as she died many decades later even though they had both been so filled up with scars and stories, they hurt each other and hardly knew each other.

And then I want the dads to be in the room and for now, for a moment, for a while, for as long as it takes, I want these mums, with their teeth and with their bare hands, and with their nails, to go unjudged, to be indulged, to be allowed, as they, as we, bite bloodied chunks out of the dads. Tear at their skin, scream into their faces, spit their blood over them.

Then I want us – me and her and her and her – to make a circle and for the dads to be in the centre, trying to have opinions about us, trying to tell stories of how 'mad' we are and how 'dangerous' and how 'difficult' and how 'not good enough'.

I want the dads to be trying to call doctors and psychiatrists, trying to get us medicated, assessed, restrained.

And I want the doctors and psychiatrists to come to the room too, with their labels and their theories, with their talk of wombs and weakness.

And I want them all to be calling to each other, comparing notes on just how bad they think we are, just how like their own terrible mums and their awful exes. I want them to be describing how good we should be, to be holding up charts with descriptions of decent and sane women and for them to be showing in graphic detail just how short we are falling, but I want their words to be impossible to hear, because we, my mum and her mum and her and her will be making a low, dark, groaning sound that will come from the stretched and scarred pit of our stomachs, which will then turn into one long, low note, so loud you might wet yourself on hearing it. So that the dads and the doctors can say 'She's mad' and 'She is weak' and 'She', 'This woman', 'This mother' 'She is the problem' as many times as they want but nobody will know or care because their voices will be impossible to hear.

My dad's mum can come too. She must. I didn't know her, but I want her with us. Born in Lancashire, worked in a mill from the age of thirteen, married by nineteen, given birth to three babies by the time she was twenty-two. Two that died and the third that lived, that one being my dad.

But she was just too full by the time he was born, full with death, with grief and with shame. That gritty grey ash type of shame that covers everything, and it had whispered to her that her babies had died because of her, because she had a bad body, because she wasn't a good enough mother.

Three times her body had not been her own, three times she'd been pregnant, her skin stretching and tearing with it, her ankles aching from carrying her own bodyweight with her babies. Joints so swollen, her wedding ring cut into the base of her finger, and the blood trickled down to her wrist.

Three times she filled up with hormones so strong they could make a person hurt themselves or bite the head off something she loved. Three times she built a body inside her own. Three times she gave birth to it, her muscles and skin ripping and contracting, causing her so much pain it felt like her arms were tied by ropes to two trucks pulling in opposite directions, tearing her in half.

Two times her baby had been dead within days, and she'd been left with breasts aching full of useless milk that she had to squeeze into an old bottle and throw down the drain.

Her body bruised and another baby to bury.

Then a baby lived, and she did try.

She tried to feed him and soothe him and wake when he needed her, despite her own desperate need to sleep.

To rock him and sing to him despite her own desperate need to scream.

But she was just too full of the wrong things, and although she tried, she couldn't take care of him in the calm, milky, warm way that a mother should. And the rage came, and the tears came, and she had the urge to bite herself and others. And her husband tutted at her and called her weak and so did his mother. (She can't come to the room, although I'm sure she has a story, but some women take sides and turn against other women and blame them and call them mad, or tell them they are not the right sort of women, that they are not woman enough or less than a woman should be, and those women can't come, those women have chosen where they stand, and if they want to tear at skin and scream they will have to make a different choice.)

And so, she, my dad's mum, rocked her living baby and tried to sing but only felt she was failing, failing at stopping babies from dying and failing at caring for them when they lived. So, one evening she went upstairs and she tried to smother her living baby intending to then end her own life, but her husband and his mother found her and took her baby from her and called her wicked, and she picked up a nearby wooden floor brush that she used to scrub the fire grate and she threw it at them. And they called her mad and they called an asylum and the asylum quickly sent a black van with no windows and it took her away and they locked her up and they cut bits out of her brain and electrocuted her and the doctors gave her state of mind long psychiatric labels, which they wrote on charts that they put at the end of her bed, but those labels were never 'bereaved' or 'poor' or 'too young' or 'sad' or 'mother' or 'tired' or 'broken-hearted'.

And she lived in the asylum until she was seventy. And she never saw her son again and nearly all her life he hated her, even though he never knew her, because he had been told a story and the story said that no good mother leaves their baby just because she cannot cope.

And the story filled him up and wiped out any other.

Being a mother is a gift, it's an honour, a privilege.

But she had ignored all that because was mad, she had abandoned him.

And decades later, when she was an old, old lady and he was a man and also a father, with the help of nurses from the asylum she found his address and wrote to him and said she loved him and that she was proud of him for the things the nurses had found out about him for her, like his work, and his family and his home and him having a good life despite having had such a bad mother. And she said that she hoped one day they could meet.

But the story he had been told had done its damage and taken root in him, the way stories do, and he couldn't let a new one in and so he never answered her letter.

And when she died and her sister wrote him another (she can come to the room, she has a story and she tried to help her sister) – when she wrote to him telling him his mum had died and asking if he would like to attend the funeral, he said he didn't want to.

And so only her sister and two nurses from the asylum went, one of them reading out a short piece where she called his mum 'a quiet, kind lady with a good sense of a humour', who was also a 'talented pianist'.

And after her sister died, nobody ever visited her grave again or even knows where it is.

So my Dad's mum must come.

And her sister must come.

And any person who has felt their body ripped in two, and has then been hated for it. They must come.

And any person who feels the need to tear at skin and scream into the face of a label, they must come.

And any person who has been called mad when what they really were was angry. Come.

And any person who has been told they are weak when what they really are is exhausted, they must come.

They all must come.

I want them all to come.

And I will hold their hands along with my own mum's hand, and hers and hers and theirs and theirs. And together we will bite and tear and rip until we are sure, and together we will groan and wail and howl, until we feel free, until we are ready to begin again, until our voices turn to thunder.

Until there is a new story.

I am running.

49

WHEN I WAS ABOUT ELEVEN, MUM WAS SICK, OR THAT'S how it was described to me.

Her own mum had just died; they'd had a 'difficult relationship'. But when it came to her mother dying, Mum had cared for her, visiting her nightly in a hospice run by nuns in a dark Victorian building on Bethnal Green Road. She often took me with her, and I'd watch as my mum carefully brushed the hair and teeth of this fragile dying woman that she had talked so many times of disliking.

But as soon as that was over, she came home and got into bed still in her clothes and went to sleep, only coming out to make food for me and to send me to school, and some days doing neither of those things. When I went in to try to talk to her, she just turned her face to the wall and said, 'Let me sleep.'

I kept saying, 'I can sleep with you, Mum.'

But she called my dad, and he came and took me away.

He said his home wasn't suitable – he had a new family by then and they needed something else – so we went to the sea, to a small flat owned by a friend of his. It was made for holidays and the sofa was covered in stiff leather that squeaked when you sat on it. It might have been a nice place in the summer, but this was winter. Dad was awkward. Didn't know what to talk about with me, and for long parts of the day he said nothing while I watched TV or wrote stories on a pad he'd given me, with squares on the paper that I spent hours turning into checks by colouring in every other one. He wasn't sure what to do when I needed a wash or how to tell me it was time to go to bed. We ate in cafés, mainly chips and puddings.

One of the days we went to the beach and sat on the cold shingle and watched a cloud of birds flying over the pier. The birds all moved at exactly the same time, a big black dotted shape, swirling and changing direction in an instant. It was the sort of thing you want to watch forever. We decided it looked like a fingerprint, the kind the police take when they arrest you, but a huge flying one. Dad knew about them. He'd never shared his knowledge with me. He said he hadn't realized I would be interested, but that day I said I was and so he told me the birds were called starlings and from a distance they look black but close up they have hundreds of iridescent coloured feathers and white spots.

The fingerprint flying only happens in autumn, just before sunset, and nobody really knows how they all understand which way to turn and when. People think they form such big groups to keep each other safe from predators, like hawks and falcons, and that they are often seen over piers because there are small fish feeding on the barnacles and seaweed on the structure in the sea below.

He told me it's called a 'murmuration', and we laughed about that and wondered if it's because, while they fly, they all murmur to each other: 'Oi! Left a bit, right a bit, not that way, you idiot!'

It's the most brilliant thing to see. And if ever I do, I think of Dad. And it's a sad feeling. Like an aching wish to return to a place I've never been.

50

'VE RUN TO THE PARK WHERE THE STUPID WOMAN'S FAT DOG growled, and the policeman said, 'Not good things, madam,' and I saw the body bag.

It's getting dark now, or as dark as it gets in a city. The sun is gone, and the sky is a milky brown fug. The gates of the park are locked. On a bench in the street nearby three young women sit huddled, smoking, laughing and telling stories.

'And I said to him, I said, "You don't respect me, so I don't respect you."'

'What? You really not gonna see him any more?'

'Nah, fuck that! I'll see him but he knows where I stand now.'

They high-five each other and shriek approval.

I'm staring at them, listening. One of them glances at me, then takes a longer look. We lock eyes for a minute. I need to bite. I could bite her. She looks like she'd bite back. We could chew chunks out of each other.

'Yeah? What are you staring at?' she says, leaning forward

towards me, away from her friends. 'What you staring at, bitch?'

We could tear each other's hearts out, set fire. I step towards her.

She goes to stand. One of the others nudges her. 'You listening? Fuck her, listen to me, this story is good, fucking focus . . .'

The young woman unlocks her gaze from mine, tuts at me and turns back to her friends.

I stand for a moment, feeling my heart in my chest thumping like a warning.

A phone goes off in her pocket and the other women's faces light up, wanting to know who it is. 'Don't fucking answer . . . Let him wait . . . Make him suffer . . .'

But she answers and immediately her voice softens. She turns her face away from her friends. 'Hello, yeah . . . Nowhere. Just out.' She stands.

'Oi, wanker! You don't deserve her!' one of the other women shouts. The one on the phone angrily waves a hand at her while walking somewhere quieter, not even noticing me now. She stops and leans on a tree trunk, her voice dissolving into treacle, smooth and shy.

'Yeah, just out . . . with mates . . . Noooo, just mate mates . . .'

I am watching her.

She notices me again and seems caught between wanting to stay soft for him and wanting to lash out at me.

I don't move.

'Yeah . . . I know you wanted to see me, but last night was like . . . Well . . . No, I'm not saying that . . . I just felt a bit . . . You were quite . . . Yeah . . . I know you like

me . . . Yeah, I know you didn't mean to . . . Look, can
you hang on a minute?'

She puts her hand over the phone and turns to me, her
voice catching fire the minute she opens her mouth, treacle
to steel. 'Can you fucking move on, please? I'm having a
private conversation here.'

I don't move.

'What the fuck is your problem?'

Through the phone his voice calling out, 'Hey . . . You
still there? Hey . . .'

She lifts it back to her ear and speaks to him, treacle
and steel now mixing. 'Just wait, eh . . . I'm dealing with
something . . .'

And back to me. Fire. 'What's fucking wrong with you?'

'You should listen to your friends.' My voice has years
and years of thunder in it.

His voice continues to call from her phone, urgent,
demanding: 'Hey, oi! What you doing!? You still there?'

She tuts at me again, shakes her head, then into her
phone, attempting treacle, but it's fading. 'Wait, will you?'

I'm still watching her.

'How can you fucking know what I should do? How can
you fucking know anything about my business? What the
fuck do you know about me?'

And he calls, 'Hey! What you doing? Oi! You there or
what?!'

I turn and walk away from her.

51

UNTIL THEY WERE ABOUT TEN, RECENT ENOUGH I CAN STILL feel it, if I lay face down on my tummy to rest – on the grass, our sofa, the kitchen floor, my bed – they would climb on top of me and lie flat, their belly along my spine, front of their knees in the backs of mine, their face turned sideways so their cheek rested on the back of my head. As if they were a blanket, as if I was a mattress, as if we were shells that fitted inside each other.

The weight, as they grew, often meant I couldn't breathe. Even when they were little my chest sometimes felt compressed. I felt like I might just crumble and become soil. Might dissolve into the earth below us and be gone. Sometimes I had to count in my head to stop myself shouting, 'Get the fuck off me!' Sometimes the counting failed, and I did shout, and they recoiled as if blasted by dynamite. Then I would feel bad and know we couldn't go back in time and that we'd both remember the shout more than the close spooned moment before it.

Now I ache for them to climb onto my back, or as they

are nearly as tall as me these days, maybe I could climb onto theirs.

Maybe if I did, they could take off, leave the ground. Maybe I could hold on around their neck and we could fly again. To a new place with different ideas, where biting and being covered in scars is understood and you don't have to hide. To a place where nobody is afraid of the worst of you, so the impulse to rip skin simply evaporates, gone, burst and vanished, like a bubble landing on concrete.

Can I climb on your back, please?

Don't grow older and find others to comfort you and to lie like shells with you.

Don't leave me – take me with you.

But a child shouldn't have to carry their parent on their back.

My mother asked me to carry her, and it didn't feel good. She was heavy, and instead of swimming I went under. Instead of flying I stayed grounded.

So, when you choose to fly, however far away, I must let you. And I must not ask for anything more.

5²

I WALK ALONG THE PARK RAILINGS, TRAILING MY FINGERS ALONG them like a stick.

I smell the air. Smell into the park. Smell the mud and the dried dog shit. I lean my head between two railings. Adjust my eyes to see through the dark. Looking for the police tape, a chalked outline of a body drawn on the ground. A 'Missing' poster. A 'Wanted' poster. A greying photograph of my face taped to a tree with red writing under it that says, 'If you see this woman, approach with caution.' Or 'Do not approach this woman: just call this number.' Or simply 'This woman is not a good woman.'

But there's nothing. No tape, no outline of a body, no cordoned-off area. Just the sound of someone crying coming from an open window down the street and the young women on the bench laughing.

53

WHAT HAD I EXPECTED?

I thought just the act of having a baby, being pregnant all those months, attending yoga classes to ensure a natural birth, going to those breastfeeding classes where we sat in a circle on hard chairs and nursed plastic dolls, I thought having small piles of neatly folded baby grows, I thought packing a 'hospital bag', equipping a changing table, having a large packet of wet wipes and a big bag of muslin cloths, I thought buying a second-hand Moses basket which my mum made a quilted fabric cover for with a pattern of vines and bright green leaves, I thought patting my tummy and playing it music and saying sorry to it when I shouted, I thought keeping my feet up, trawling second-hand shops for tiny vintage dungarees like the ones I'd worn as a child, I thought buying handcrafted wooden blocks and not plastic ones, I thought having *The Very Hungry Caterpillar* and *In the Night Kitchen* on the shelf and a book about courageous parenting, I thought a bedside light in the shape of a mushroom, I thought a sheepskin

– actually two, one for the pram and one for the Moses basket, I thought a baby-carrier in soft purple corduroy that I could strap tightly to my chest so they would hear my heart beating and would feel like they were still in the womb, I thought an octopus with a rattle in every tentacle apart from the one that was a squeaker, I thought the large-size tub of Sudocrem, I thought going to talks on vaccines run by the women who taught the yoga where I had to pretend I believed in homeopathy in order to fit in, I thought fighting to get them into the best school, I thought getting their teeth checked regularly, I thought a yearly summer holiday and day trips to the sea, I thought letting them sleep on my chest all night, I thought letting them sleep in my bed when they had bad dreams, I thought feeding through the pain, I thought standing at the park gates just before sunrise, them in their buggy wrapped up warm and wide awake while I was half asleep waiting for the gates to open so they could go on the swings and I could push them and hope they would laugh, I thought hiring child-minders who were kinder and more patient than me, I thought finding a man, I thought changing their school when a child kept hitting them in the back when they turned away, I thought changing their school again when a teacher kept giving them sad-face stickers on the chart of 'good behaviour', I thought complaining about the headmistress who called their art homework 'derivative', I thought making sure their shoes fitted, I thought making sure they put a coat on when it was cold, I thought chasing them to put suntan cream on when it was hot, I thought trying to talk to the mothers of their friends even though I had nothing in common with them, I thought getting them a good mattress, a good desk, the right chair, a good pair of snow boots, sandals that didn't rub, I thought telling their father to see them more, I thought telling lies to protect them, I thought telling them the truth so they didn't suspect something was going on but feel too scared to ask about it, I thought telling them it was OK to hate me, I thought white-noise machines, I thought birthday parties with hired clowns, cakes in the shape of things they loved, hiring a tutor because I lacked the knowledge they needed, I thought an old wooden sledge like the ones in Christmas cards, I thought the paediatrician with the very long waiting list, I thought buying vegetables and not too many sweets, I thought sometimes letting them just eat sweets, I thought making a roast, I thought trips to the zoo, I thought being called Mum, I thought being called a woman, I thought wanting not to be like my own mum, I thought loving them so much I can't describe it, I thought wanting . . .

I was stupid.

54

THE POLICE STATION IS QUIET.

A woman in uniform behind the desk is chatting to a man who is obviously a plain-clothes policeman – too much gold jewellery, an orange and green Hawaiian shirt under a stiff black leather jacket. A ridiculous outfit. They both have cups of tea and are talking about holidays. Posters along the walls about what to do if you see a crime, what to do if you're the victim of one, nothing about being the perpetrator.

I stand in the doorway waiting to be noticed.

He tells her about a trip he once made to a place where you could jump off a bridge wearing a harness so you didn't hit the water and instead you just sort of hurtled towards it, then at the last minute dangled above it. 'The buzz! The fucking buzz, near death but not.'

She tells him she's always wanted to go to Las Vegas. He asks if she's a gambler. She replies, 'I dabble but I know when to stop.'

I cough. They both turn round.

'Can I help you?' she asks.

I step towards them.

'You OK?' she asks, in a voice that lets me know she wishes I wasn't there.

'I'll leave you to it,' he says to her. 'See you later.'

As he carries his tea he uses his foot to kick open the double doors behind her desk, which swing shut behind him, like a cowboy has just entered a saloon.

'What do you need?' she asks, her eyes glancing back to where he just was.

'I want to ask about the body in the park.'

She looks at me blankly. 'What body in what park?'

'This morning there was a body bag in the park.'

I hold out my hands fingernail side up.

'A boy went missing at my child's school. I think there was a toe on our doorstep. I'm worried it was me. I can do terrible things. I think it might have been me.'

She is about to speak when behind me the door from the street flies open and two men come in, one clutching his head, blood on his face, blood on his hands and down the front of his shirt and trousers; he even has blood on his shoes. The other man, who has grazed bloodied knuckles that he doesn't try to hide, shouts past me to the officer, 'Stupid fucking wanker walked into a wall. Don't blame me. He's a stupid fuck.'

He glances at me, his eyes hard and cold, like dirt trapped under ice. 'All right, love, no need to stare.' Then back to the officer. 'He needs a fucking ambulance. I'm not doing it. You lot need to sort it. I'm not a fucking Samaritan.'

The officer goes to answer him, but he waves a dismissive hand in her direction while pushing past me to dump the bloodied man onto a chair where he lands with a heavy thump. The man with the knuckles tells him again he's a stupid fucking wanker, tells the officer to call an ambulance, barks at me to cheer up, adding that if I smiled more I might get a husband, kicks open the door and leaves.

The officer looks to me and shakes her head.

From his chair the bloodied man begins to mumble. 'Cunt. Stupid cunt.'

'That's enough of that language,' the officer tells him sternly while pressing a bell in front of her, which can then be heard ringing in the offices behind. 'If you men need an ambulance you need to call it yourselves, I'm not your mummy.' She looks at me, shakes her head again and rolls her eyes.

Behind her the bell carries on ringing, calling out for help that isn't coming.

55

MY MUM WROTE A LETTER FOR ME TO READ AFTER SHE WAS dead.

It said things about how she had chosen to die and how I might feel guilty about having let her. It told me not to. Said other things about the indignities of ageing, talked about being released from them. At the end it said, 'I regret so much of our life together. I was an inadequate parent, only half formed myself.'

56

THE DOOR BEHIND THE FEMALE OFFICER CLANGS OPEN, TWO male officers, one older, full of just being him, a button on his shirt popped open so his hairy, tightly rounded tummy is exposed. The other man is young, wide-eyed. A cliché. Spots and a smell of fresh. The older one bangs his hand down on the bell, so the ringing comes to an abrupt halt.

'You called?' he says to the female officer in a funny voice, taking the piss, showing off his lack of concern.

She nods to the bloodied man now slumped in the chair rolling a cigarette, covering his papers in blood and dirt. 'Said we have to call him an ambulance.'

'Does he now?'

'And her?' They look to me.

I am sitting next to the bloodied man, staring at a poster about car theft. A shape of a person with long spiked fingers is opening a car door – they don't even have a face.

'No smoking.' the female officer snaps at the man.

'Fuck off,' he says.

'Wish I could,' she answers, 'but I'm telling you, you better not light that.'

She looks to me. 'Do you want to tell them why you're here, love? She said something about a body bag.'

57

THERE ARE MOMENTS, AMONG ALL THE REPAIRING AND craving, aching to be different, when me and them curl up next to each other and they point at my scars, tracing them with their fingers and they ask me about them. And I can face the stories without the screaming urge to apologize again or beg forgiveness.

And we tell stories of biting and ripping and dead things, stories about me and what I have done, and what we have recovered from and will no doubt continue to.

And while we talk, we laugh and we think and we catch sight of the way we have grown and adapted, we can name the harm that has been caused without causing more, we talk about other people that we see who also have scars that they can trace with their fingers. And we talk about how we know that even though it hurts, and it definitely hurts, we do understand dads who leave, who don't call, who don't seem to see their effect, dads who swallowed dangerous stories whole and didn't even try to consider new ones until it was, perhaps, too late. We admit that we understand the dads who call their mums and the mums of their children mad, because we know how powerful stories can be and we see those dads have scars of their own.

And this story makes sense to us.

And this story is of value.

This story expands our world instead of shrinking it.

Instead of it just being the story about the awful hopeless mother and her poor child.

Or the terrible father and all that he neglected.

58

THE OFFICER HAS BROUGHT ME A TEA.

They did call an ambulance for the bloodied man – he made a fuss when it arrived, suddenly crying and showing his wounds, telling us a long, complicated story about a woman and money, a baby, a broken promise and many, many more cunts. The paramedics talked to him like he was a child who wouldn't go to bed, saying things to him like 'Yes, yes' and 'You need to stop crying now' and 'That's enough for one night'.

As he was leaving, he told the female officer that he loved her and that she was an angel. She tutted and told him to behave himself.

The older officer is sitting opposite me. Leaning forward so that the button on his shirt gapes open even more and his whole belly button is now sticking out, like it's about to blow me a kiss. The younger officer is sitting next to me, awkward.

We've been talking for a while. The old officer asked why I'd come. I told him I was worried that I'd killed someone. The missing boy. I told him I was scared it had been me. I told him I'd seen a body bag.

I'd started to cry and said things about not being a good person, knowing I was a bad one; he'd gestured for the younger officer to get a tissue. Which he did and which is now crumpled in my fist. He'd asked me which school my child goes to and I'd given the name. He'd asked my name and I'd given that.

He'd told me to stay where I was. Then he'd gone out past the female officer and through the cowboy-saloon double doors, sharing a joke with her as he did that made them both glance in my direction.

While he was gone the young officer and the female officer started to talk about a works party that they'd been invited to and the fact they thought it was unfair they were having to pay for their own drinks.

I sat staring at another poster, for something called Mental Health Day: it had a picture of a brain with a large open mouth just about to swallow a stick person and above that there was the instruction not to believe everything you think.

When he came back, he'd brought me the tea and his shirt button had been done up.

And now he is sitting opposite me, using my name as if he knows me.

As if he knows all about me.

'No dead boy.'

He hands me a small brown stained packet of sugar and a plastic stick for stirring.

I look at him. I don't take the sugar.

'But the school called. My child had to come home.'

'Yep. But no dead boy.'

'They said he was missing.'

'And he was. But he's home now. You should put sugar in it. It tastes like metal and piss. It's an old kettle.'

'But they said . . .'

'Had a row with his parents or something. Wanted to scare them. Which he did. And you by the look of things. But he's home now, no doubt bed with no dinner.'

'But I saw a body bag. There was a body. In the park. This morning.'

'Parks can be full of bodies in the morning. People do all sorts of terrible shit. Isn't that right?'

He looks at the younger officer who nods obligingly as if he isn't certain of what he's nodding about, while the female officer leans forward and repeats what he's said in full agreement.

'Terrible shit. All sorts.'

'But I saw a toe, it still had blood. I covered it in leaves. My child . . .'

He leans further forward so the button on his shirt slides open once more and his belly button gasps for air.

And he says my name again, his voice like a cloud wrapped in bricks. 'You tell us you've done something awful. You tell us you aren't a good person.'

Falling. I'm falling again.

'But I'm not. I'm not a good person.'

I hold out my hands to him, wanting him to look at my nails. Wanting him to see the blood, but he doesn't look.

'You're not a murderer, though, are you?'

And, for a moment . . .

'Where's your child?'

'At home.'

'Alone?'

'With a friend.'

'Are they safe?'

We both pause.

'Do you want us to take you home? I think we should. I think you should go home.'

He stands. Looks down at my feet.

I look at them.

My feet are bare. I hadn't realized. I must have jumped and run with no shoes. My feet are covered in dirt and there's blood. Blood between my toes and under my nails.

59

I WAS BIG WHEN I WAS PREGNANT.

They were not a big baby when they were born, but I was swelling with it, bursting with it, wanted it to be seen. I must be a good person. Only good women can be pregnant.

I liked when people smiled at me in that gentle way they do at pregnant women, or some pregnant women, the 'right' kind. I looked like the right kind. Maybe a bit young but that was only sweeter. And I would smile back as if I was now transformed and only ever gentle. It wasn't true but it felt like it should be.

I signed up to a yoga class for expecting mums. We took our shoes off together in the carpeted hallway and smiled at each other as we waddled in our socks into a large room swaddled in the smell of incense with wooden Buddhas and yellow walls, with mats and folded blankets laid out ready for us on the shiny wooden floor.

The teacher was an expert in natural birth, a rake-thin older woman with wild, greying hair, velvet leggings and a smoky voice. She told us about oils to rub on our tummies and teas to drink to make our vaginas supple and ready for birthing. She gave us postures to do to help our babies drop; she laid lavender-scented beanbags on our eyelids as we lay on our backs and breathed. She squeezed the soles of our feet as if we deserved it.

I went every week and I felt like I belonged. I believed my birth would be natural, I rubbed my tummy with the oils, I drank the tea, I ached for her foot squeezes and melted when they came.

My stomach was so big that when I sat on the floor with my legs outstretched it was like I had a planet lying on my thighs. My very own planet. I could rest my head on it and hear our hearts.

I felt filled to the brim with the possibility of being a different me. A better one.

I lay with the beanbags over my eyes and believed it was the truth. After the class we sat in a circle, like precious urns, drinking the right tea and talking about our birth plans, resting our hands on our tummies and patting them as we talked in our gentle vessel voices. Gentle women. Gentle, pregnant, good women, ready to burst and become the good, gentle mums we were destined to be.

After my birth, when the closest I got to a 'natural birth' was being pushed at speed in a wheelchair past the room where the proper women were having water births, I tried a few baby-massage classes run by the same yoga lady. But the atmosphere was very different. Those who were coping very much separate from those who weren't. My baby cried and wriggled like an oiled fish, then did a poo on the blanket, which I'd had to borrow as I'd forgotten to bring my own. I swore and a few women tutted.

I wanted to bite the teacher who had told us all that shit about oils and teas and supple vaginas and breathing.

But I was too tired to even bite, so I just said it had all been 'amazing' and other women nodded back with smiles I couldn't read.

I wanted us to howl together, to scream at the sky, to admit that the incense-yoga-mat fantasy of how it was going to be had evaporated, no, had been blasted, bombed, smashed into how it actually was, and that our shelves with all the books on perfect-imperfect yet actually pretty perfect parenting and how to achieve ideal sleep patterns and our cupboards filled with the right oils and the good teas looked down on us, disappointed, as we staggered and stuttered and rattled, bemused and battered, through our days, wiping up shit and sick, bleeding and leaking into our pants and bras, trudging behind buggies, bleary and sleep-deprived.

But the other women, who'd spoken so openly about their plans and their tea and their supple perineums before our births, were now closed, shut up, like boarded-over shop windows. Each now in her own world, totally alone, not letting anyone know how she really felt or whether she was actually coping. No longer bonded by our tummies. None of us feeling safe enough to admit that, despite the flowery teas and the yoga poses, each screaming shit-stained day we drifted further away from being the natural perfect earth mother that had so very recently felt like an incense-smelling certainty.

60

THE POLICE CAR SMELLS OF DISINFECTANT. THE OLD OFFICER with the tummy is driving, beside him the young one. They gave me blue plastic bags to wear on my feet, like hairnets. My toes clenched and cold inside them, like the body in the bag that they say I didn't see.

I'm in the back seat, facing the window, looking out.

'You OK back there?' he asks routinely, his kindness well rehearsed.

'I'm fine,' I reply, no point in any other answer.

The car turns a corner, the shitty park drifts past beside me, the old bike locks dangling.

'This is the park,' I say.

They both ignore me.

On the bench where the young women were, just the one woman is left, her friends have gone, and in their place a young man. He is standing in front of her, she is seated, and he is shouting. But she is shouting back. And she looks strong.

I watch for a while, hearing his words carrying on the wind. And I think he is saying he is sorry.

I turn and look through the window on the other side of the car, to the park. All along the railings, I think I can see shapes, outlines – like the car thief in the poster at the police station – shapes of figures, their backs to us.

I slide myself across the seat to get a better view. Yes, I saw shapes. Holding onto the bars, the way desperate prisoners do in bad films. Leaning into the dark, the way I had.

More mothers. More women. More people. More. More of us. Looking for clues. Looking for proof.

We drive down the road where my child's friend ran from us. Lying on a wall, its stomach to the sky being stroked by a passer-by, is the tabby cat.

'Which one is yours?' he asks, from the front seat.

A mother shouldn't be delivered home in a police car.

Not bare feet in a police car.

That wasn't in any of the parenting books. Not the one on how to talk so children will listen, not the one on letting them sleep in your bed, not the one on them deciding when the breastfeeding ends, not the one on being conscious, not the one on being unconditional, not the one you would wish your own parents had read, not the one about how the French bring up children who never throw food, not the one on how to never have a 'bad child', not the one about the 'explosive child' or 'the spirited child', not the one on how to raise an adult for success, not the one on how to raise a good man, not the one on how to raise girls who aren't mean, not the one on how to parent from the inside out, not the one on how to be mindful while mothering, not the A to Z of, not the handbook of, not the bible of.

I didn't ignore the books. I read the books. I read them and I still bit through bone. I still ripped at skin and tore holes in walls. I still shouted till they cried, I still feared their need, I still neglected them, I still couldn't be consistent. 'Good' mothering followed 'bad' and 'bad' wiped out 'good'. Rebuild, start over, make the same mistake, start again, stay again, run away, come back again, try again, mess it up again.

The books didn't ever tell me what to do after I had torn through muscle with my teeth, spat blood into my sink, chewed on the door of my locked room till I knocked out a tooth, then made a packed lunch, washed a uniform, read a story, and returned to tearing at my own arms.

'Do you live here?' he asks again.

The police car is outside my home. Our home.

'Yes.' I say. 'This is where we live.'

I am standing on our doorstep. The police car drives away. Before he goes, he leans out of the window and tells me to 'Have a bath and a cup of tea.' And the young man beside him just nods.

I look up to see a neighbour's face dart away from her window. I growl. With the blue plastic bags still on my feet, I kick at the leaves looking for the toe. I can't find it, just the discarded wrapper of some sweets that I pick up and chuck into the bin along with the blue bags.

Barefoot, I ring our bell.

My child's voice through the intercom: 'Yes? Hello?'

'It's me, love.'

'Mum!' They buzz me in.

The flat is quiet; they've tidied. The lights are dimmed, low like they know I like them.

'I wish you wouldn't run like that, Mum.'

'I know, I'm so sorry,' I say. 'Where's your friend?'

Their light in the shape of a moon is on but dimmed to just an orangey glow. She is asleep again, curled up in their bed.

They whisper, their voice full of pride, something maternal in it. 'I gave her some of your pyjamas, Mum. I hope that's OK.'

'Of course.'

'I made her a hot chocolate the way you do with the froth stuff, Mum. I used a fork – I couldn't find the whisk thing. It worked really well.'

'That's brilliant, my love. Where will you sleep?'

They gesture for me to be quiet, closing the door on their friend the way you close a door after you've finally got a baby to sleep.

In the sitting room the sofa has been made up as a bed. The duvet turned down and inviting, the way they do in hotels. A pillow has been plumped, a blanket laid over for warmth. 'I made it,' they tell me. 'Looks comfortable, eh?'

'Very,' I say.

They look down at my feet. 'You need to wash your feet, Mum.'

I nod. But I don't move. 'You said a thing, love . . .' I venture, tentative. But I can see I am about to break the mood, the one they have so lovingly created, and their face drops from pride to wariness.

'Just leave it . . . can we, can we not?'

'Let me just ask, love.'

They look at me, a flash of anger but I push on. 'You said you were like me. Earlier, you said, "I'm like you." What did you mean?'

They scrunch up their face the way they used to when they were tiny and I gave them something to eat that they didn't like the taste of.

'Why did you say that?'

'Oh, I dunno. Sometimes. I dunno. I'm a bit like you. I don't know what I meant.'

'But in what ways?' I ask.

'Mum, fuck's sake, I dunno.' Desperate for me to leave them be.

But I don't move. So, they talk hoping it's enough for me.

'OK, you make really nice beds when people come to stay. You make really good hot chocolate when I can't sleep. You make nice food. And sometimes you get really fucking angry. Sometimes I am a bit like you, that's all I meant. OK? Enough? Wash your feet, Mum, they're disgusting.'

Again I don't move. Now I am the one talking. 'I'm so sorry, I want to be better. I will never stop trying to be better. I am so sorry I hurt you.'

'I know, Mum. I know that. Please. Leave it. The bed looks good, doesn't it?'

'It does,' I say. 'But, my love, please know, I am so, so sorry . . . so . . .'

'Please, Mum, please stop saying sorry. Please, enough. It's too much.'

And so I do. I stop. I swallow my sorry down, knowing it is mine to carry forever in the pit of my stomach like another child.

And I go to wash my feet.

61

WHEN THEY WERE BORN THE NURSE HANDED THEM TO ME and laid them on my chest. Both naked, our skin touching. My body ripped and bleeding. Their tiny body covered in blood and mucus.

I was terrified. I felt like I was the tiny one and that they were so much bigger than I could ever be.

Our hearts beating together.

I stroked their hand, and they took hold of my finger, their whole hand holding on tight. Unexpectedly strong.

Like I was a tree trunk.

Like I was their mum.

Acknowledgements

I have lived my own version of some of the experiences that I have fictionalised here. Personal experience was my reason to write, an attempt to voice those thoughts and feelings it is often not easy to give voice to.

But my having some personal proximity to this story means that those close to me also do. So, I would like to acknowledge and thank them for their acceptance and understanding, along with all those who supported me in the writing and publishing of this book.